D1167598

The Lamp
of
Umm Hashim
and other Stories

The Lamp
of
Umm Hashim
and other Stories

Yahya Hakki

Translated by
Denys Johnson-Davies

The American University in Cairo Press
Cairo   New York

Contents

Translator's
Introduction

Yahya Hakki (1905–90) was one of that small group of out-
standing talents that laid the foundations for a literary renaissance of Arabic literature in Egypt around the middle of
the twentieth century. Other writers who participated in
that renaissance included the scholar and man of letters
Taha Hussein, the playwright Tewfik al-Hakim, the pioneer
writer of the short story Mahmoud Teymour, and, of course,
the novelist Naguib Mahfouz.

Yahya Hakki's works number several volumes of short stories and critical writings, including a short book about the
Egyptian short story. He was also influential in the encour-
agement he gave to younger writers through his personal
contacts with them and his position as editor of the literary
monthly *al-Magalla*, which he edited with flair and imagination for many years. The present volume contains a few
examples of his output in the field of fiction, among them

his longest and best known work, the novella "The Lamp of Umm Hashim," first published in 1944. This was the first fictional work in Arabic to deal with the psychological difficulties that were faced by students returning home after being sent to Europe to complete their studies. Though published more than half a century ago, it can still be read with pleasure, for the themes around which it revolves—as summed up in Kipling's lines about east and west never being able to meet—are still relevant. The novella tells the story of a young man who, after financial sacrifices by his father, goes to England to pursue his medical studies. He comes from a conservative family and is torn between the new influences to which he is exposed in England, including a love affair with an English girl, and his own religious upbringing. On his return to Cairo, this struggle is epitomized when he has to treat the eye complaint of Fatima, his cousin and bride-to-be; the novella recounts his attempts to reconcile the scientific knowledge he has acquired in the west with the superstitious beliefs held by his own mother and the inhabitants of the poor district in which he decides to practice medicine. "The Lamp of Umm Hashim" was recognized as being a sophisticated work of fiction for its time, and other novels dealing with similar themes soon followed, notably Tewfik al-Hakim's *'Asfur min al-sharq* ('Bird from the East') and, later, the more explicit *Mawsim al-hijra ila-l-shamal (Season of Migration to the North)* by the Sudanese Tayeb Salih.

Early on in his career as a lawyer—he was later to become a diplomat and to spend several periods serving both in the Arab world and in Europe—Yahya Hakki worked for some time in Upper Egypt, where he came to have an affectionate understanding for the peasants who labor under its scorching sun and harsh conditions. His "Story from Prison" makes up a threesome of longer stories about Upper Egypt in a volume entitled *Blood and Mud*. The story, like many of his writings, deals with characters who, despite being the very backbone of the country, feature all too seldom in the literature of Egypt—in fact, this is not peculiar to Arabic writing, for peasants in general rate scarcely a mention in world literature. Hakki, however, possessed in marked degree a sympathetic rapport with the underdog, combined with an ability to depict, in a way that was not at all condescending, characters from the humbler walks of life. This can be seen in the short story "Mother of the Destitute," in which he creates an atmosphere not dissimilar to that of his novella, and where the 'chorus' to this fable-story is composed of that mass of teeming humanity that crowd the square in which so much of the action occurs. The very early and very short "Story in the Form of a Petition," which I first translated and published locally in Cairo in the 1940s, shows Yahya Hakki's readiness to adopt new modes of storytelling.

When writing about peasants, as in "Story from Prison," Hakki shows how the colloquial language can be used to give an extra dimension to creative writing, in particular where dialogue in concerned. Much of the story is recounted in the words of the gipsy protagonist and shows how the writer, famed for his rich, condensed style in the classical language, was able to employ the colloquial language with equal imagination to draw a lifelike portrait of a character who would be quite incapable of expressing himself in the literary language. A degree of realism is thus achieved that would be impossible if the classical language were used exclusively for such stories. Who, it may be asked, converses in the classical language other than the characters in most Arabic novels? It is surely significant that, for instance, Tewfik al-Hakim, a leading contributor to the creation of a modern Arabic literature, also exploited the rare richness of Egypt's spoken language in many of his writings, including the novel translated under the title *Maze of Justice*; Yusuf Idris, too, a younger writer much admired by Hakki, enriched many of his short stories by drawing on his command of the colloquial language. If the criteria to be taken into consideration are purely aesthetic, then the colloquial language must surely form an additional weapon in the armory of anyone writing in Arabic. Individual writers must of course come to their own decision about this. Of the major writers in Egypt it is only Naguib Mahfouz who has turned his back on the colloquial language, though when his novels have been adapted for the screen, his characters regain their natural voices.

For a man who made his career outside academic life, Yahya Hakki was unusually widely read in the classical tradition of literature, in both poetry and prose. In his advice to younger writers he always stressed the importance of possessing a true mastery of the language in which one was seeking to convey one's thoughts. He deplored the way in which, year by year, there was a palpable decline in people's knowledge at all levels of the Arabic language. He asked that those in authority face up to the fact that Arabic, unlike European languages, possesses both a written and a spoken form; he felt the problem lay in the fact that the classical language was being taught as though it were another foreign language.

🎐

As a person, Yahya Hakki bridged east and west with ease. During his years as a diplomat he had lived abroad, only resigning from the service after marrying a Frenchwoman. This was his second marriage, for his first wife had died tragically young after giving birth to a daughter. It was thus after a short career in the law, followed by several years in the Foreign Service, that Yahya Hakki began to devote all his time to making his name as a man of letters.

Despite the difference in age, he and I became friends during the years between 1945 and 1949 when I was living permanently in Cairo and teaching at Cairo University. It seems that we both left Cairo at about the same time, for going through some old papers recently, I found a letter from him sent to me in Teheran. The letter-heading was that of the Egyptian Embassy in Paris; it was written with the same warmth and wit, in a light-hearted mixture of the classical and colloquial languages, as he used in the letters he wrote to his daughter Noha. These have been collected and published under the title *Rasa'il Yahya Haqqi ila ibnatihi* ('Yahya Hakki's Letters to His Daughter'), with an introduction by Naguib Mahfouz, who was a close friend and admirer of Hakki's and had at one time worked under him.

Before leaving Cairo in 1949 I discussed with Yahya Hakki my wish to produce a general volume of short stories in English translation that would show how the short story was being practiced throughout the Arab world. No such project had previously been undertaken and it would, I felt, do something about putting modern Arabic literature 'on the map,' especially if it were to come out from an established English publisher. So, while living outside Egypt yet paying regular visits, I would call on Yahya Hakki. On each occasion he would greet me with a mischievous smile and would inquire, like some co-conspirator, how my famous volume of Arabic short stories was faring. We both secretly shared the thought that it was little more than a pipe dream! In fact, it took some twenty years before I had gathered sufficient material for such a volume, after which I was still faced with the formidable task— for someone without the necessary contacts—of finding a publisher willing to undertake such an unusual project. Nevertheless, the day did come when, by great good fortune, I chanced upon 'someone who knew someone' at Oxford University Press. The book was accepted for publication on the understanding that it was a work of scholarship. Naturally, I did not quibble, and was delighted at being able to announce to Yahya Hakki on my next visit to Cairo that none other than OUP was to publish the volume of *Modern Arabic Short Stories.* Needless to say, it contained a story by him.

Yahya Hakki was the most caring of people, and this caring embraced people from all walks of life and extended as well to animals. This can be seen in much of his writing, as for instance in his description of the dog's death by poison in "Story from Prison." Among the aphorisms of the writer quoted in his daughter's book is this one: "I know of nothing that so completes a person's humanity as kindness to dumb animals."

I was surprised to learn, when reading recently of his early life, that he had been born of humble parents in a poor district of Cairo, and that he had experienced periods of financial hardship, especially toward the end of his long life. At one point it was suggested that his name be put up for the Saddam Hussein Prize, but he was horrified by the idea of accepting such a prize and having to shake a hand so stained by the blood of innocent Muslims. In fact, he was helped financially by the award of the King Faisal Prize, though by that time he was not fit enough to travel to Saudi Arabia to receive it.

The last occasion on which we met was when he was asked to speak at the American University in Cairo shortly after Naguib Mahfouz was awarded the Nobel prize for literature. He did not deliver a lecture but gave off-the-cuff answers to questions sent up to him on pieces of papers by members of the audience, which were then read out to him. My own question inquired how it was that Egyptians, so famed for their sense of humor, had produced little humor in their literature. He did not so much answer my question as agree with me, for he had himself, I later learned, written an essay deploring the general air of gloom that surrounds so much modern Arabic writing. I recollect that another member of the audience asked him whether he had never thought he might one day be awarded the Nobel prize. He gave that quizzical smile of his before answering that no, he had never entertained any such dream, for he was only too aware that somewhere else in Cairo there was somebody who was writing away with greater talent, dedication, and industry than himself.

He was ever the most modest of people.

The Lamp
of
Umm Hashim

Story in the Form of a Petition

Petition:

We have heard that you have forwarded, are about to forward, or will forward—and true knowledge abides in God alone—to the various countries a detailed list of losses in lives and property sustained by our beloved Egypt by reason of the war. I am sure that the name of my dear, good-hearted, and unfortunate friend, Fahmi Tawakkul Saafan, is not cited in this list, for, overcome by shyness, he would have preferred to remain silent. Were it not for my love for him and the knowledge that he has been unfairly treated, I would not trouble you with this petition, in which I ask that you include his name in the list, and that you register under the section of property, the following losses:

£E150 in bank notes

£E50—a gold cigarette case (not counting the value of the Lucky Strike in it)

£E25—A Dunhill lighter

£E50—A fourth-hand Ballila car (I am unable to estimate the age of the tires, not being an expert in antiques)

I also trust that under the section of lives lost you will place the name of my friend. Though actually still alive, he's like a dead man among the living, like a man clutching in his hand a clothing coupon for one austerity shroud.

Subject:

Fahmi Tawakkul Saafan and I were fellow students. Sitting next to each other, we became bosom friends. Later we separated, because after the Primary certificate he was forced to give up his studies owing to lack of funds; he then went off to his village, after which he returned and opened a small shop for shoe-shines in the American style. Having sufficient money, I was able to continue with my education, and then I got a job as messenger in the Post Office. The job requiring that I had my shoes cleaned every day and resoled every two weeks, the link of friendship between us was restored. I would find him sitting at a small table, behind him a raucous radio, and on his right a sewing-machine, the noise of which was interrupted by the blows of a hammer driving nails into heels and soles. He began trading in leather, and it was then that the war broke out and the money began to roll in. The thermometer by which I measured the rise in his fortunes was the cigarette he smoked: a Laziz or a Feel, then it became a Maadan or a Flag, then a Mumtaz or a Wasp. When I found him offering me a Chesterfield from a cigarette case, I knew that he had become one of the war's nouveaux riches.

I was not surprised when I found he had bought a Ballila

car, which he used to drive himself, and in which he drove to the cabaret of Lawahiz, the glamorous dancer. Falling madly in love with her and neglecting his work, he finally arrived at the best possible solution to save himself the trouble of going to the cabaret every day—this he achieved by transferring the cabaret to his bedroom: in short, he married Lawahiz, a girl possessed of a face that, when unwashed, was a masterpiece of beauty and a body that, when washed, would seduce a monk. So you see, love, besides being blind and deaf, is sometimes stricken by a cold in the nose. Said my friend: "My house became a hell. . . . The whole day long she was in her nightgown but when evening came, she dressed up, whether we were going out or not. Night was turned into day. Yawning hard, I would make a breakfast of cooked food, while lunch would consist of tea with milk.

"Hardly had she entered my house than the old servant woman, who had cooked and washed for me ever since I'd come to Cairo, took herself off. Lawahiz asked—or rather ordered—me to look for another servant. No sooner, however, had I brought a servant than she threw her out, saying she knew all about her bad character (later I discovered that she spoke from first-hand knowledge, both girls having graduated from the same domestic agency). I brought along numerous others, until I had paid the agency, in a few days, more than the wages of a servant for a whole year. In the end the doorkeeper put me on to Naima, a timid young girl with two long plaits, as clean as if she'd just come out of a bath, as well as being brought up as though she'd come from Istanbul. Lawahiz was pleased with her; she was no doubt reassured by the pigtails, which told her that Naima was not a spoiled modern servant. Naima was happy to be with us and was satisfied with her bed in the basement. But I became scared when I saw Nai'ma beginning to show affection for me: she would get my clothes ready, clean them with great pleasure, and give me the very best food, meat and fruits, glancing at me as if to say: 'Never mind—hard luck!'

"I realized how imminent the occurrence of some fresh catastrophe was, for I felt that my wife had begun to look at Naima with that eye that God has given to every woman at the back of her head. Ah! my friend, you don't know—as I do—the destruction of how many homes has begun with that sympathy generated between a persecuted husband and a kind-hearted servant. Thus it was with no rejoicing that I saw the seeds of jealousy take root in Lawahiz's heart. It is said that the manifestation of jealousy is evidence of love, but I don't believe the ravings of philosophers when they talk of jealousy, for jealousy is one thing and *love* something else. In my opinion jealousy more closely resembles those lofty emotions that stir a cat, in body, hair, paw, and claw, when it is about to eat up a mouse and finds in front of it another cat. Afraid that Naima would be thrown out and that we would return to our state of anarchy, I spent my nights in thought until the Devil inspired me with a cunning plan.

"I got up early and went round the domestic agencies in search of a chauffeur, for I had pretended to my wife that my eyes were so tired, my nerves so frayed, that I was frightened I might run someone over in crowded Farouk Street. I was offered an old driver, unassuming and honest, whom I refused; in the imploring eyes of another I discerned fear and humility, so him too I rejected, in spite of the modest wage he was asking. I refused many others, until I discovered just what I wanted: a tall, dark, broad-shouldered young man, with gray trousers, a canary yellow waistcoat, a red tie, and hair on which had been smeared a whole pot of brilliantine. He looked at me with an impudent gaze, and when he smiled, one could see that he had large, shining teeth. I was further delighted when on asking his name, he answered "At your service—Anwar." I found that his name had an attractive ring about it. I engaged him right away, handed over my car to him, and prepared him a bed in a room in the basement, right opposite Naima's.

"That night I slept happy in the thought that I had escaped from a catastrophe, that Naima's affections would be transferred from me to this Rudolf Valentino.

"A few days later, on returning home, I found neither Mr. Anwar nor the car. My plan had worked in the main though not in the details. Anwar certainly *had* fallen under a strong passion that had driven him to elope with his beloved. But it was not Naima who had fled with him, but my dear wife, Lawahiz. It was thus, also, that my money and my car took wings. No doubt the cigarette case and the lighter were her first presents to him."

In view of the above I humbly submit this my petition, trusting that you will give my friend's case your kind consideration.

Signed
Yahya Hakki

Mother
of the Destitute

◎

Praised be He whose dominion extends over all creatures
and who knows no opposition to His rule. Here I have no
wish but to recount the story of Ibrahim Abu Khalil as he
made his way down the steps of life, like the leaves of spring,
which, though lifted a little by the wind, contain even at
their height their ineluctable descent until at last they are
cushioned and trampled down into the earth. I was a witness
to his descent of the last steps of the ladder, but I learned
only later that he was an orphan and had been cast out upon
the world at an early age; as to whether he came from the
town or the country I do not know, though my belief is that
he was a city creature born and bred. His life of misery started with being a servant, then a vendor of lupine seeds on a
handcart hung round with earthenware water-coolers from
Qena, their necks decorated with flowers and sweet basil. I
heard that later he had opened a small herbalist's, after

which he had gone back again to being a street vendor, jumping from tram to tram with his pins, needles for primus stoves, and clothes pegs. His life contained sporadic periods about which I have no information, although I am inclined to think that during his roving existence he must at times have known the sting of asphalt in the Qaramaydan penitentiary.

Just before I got to know him he used to occupy the triangular corner of the sidewalk in the square facing the shop of the Turk who sold halva. There he would sit with a basket of radishes, rocket, and leeks. His cry was simply, "Tender radishes, fine rocket!" His face told of none of the various upheavals he had been through or the buffetings he had had in his innumerable occupations. Such people take life as it comes; each day has its individual destiny, each day passes away and dies—like them—without legacy. They enter life's arena with their sensitivity already dead—has it died from ignorance, from stupidity, or from contentment and acceptance? Their eyes do not even blink at the abuse showered down at them. Yet you must not be too hasty in judging in case you should be unfair; had you known him as I did you would have found him a simple-hearted person— genial, polite, and generous.

In spite of the efforts he expended in his search for sufficient food to keep himself alive, his heart knew neither envy nor rancor. His rheumy eyes hinted that in his heart there was a latent propensity for joking and being jolly. He had a most captivating way of looking at you; his smile seemed to emerge through veil after veil—just like watching a slow-motion picture of the birth of a smile of the eyes. When he raised his face, sheltering his eyes with his hand, it would seem to me as if the world had shrunk to this small frame containing just the two of us and that his words were a communion, subdued and private.

Abu Khalil would take up his accustomed place shortly before noon. When afternoon came and the morning basket was sold out, or almost so, he would get up and walk off in his languid way; wandering around the square, he would pass by many of the shopkeepers, lingering with this one and that as they asked each other how they were getting on, and swapping anecdotes and jokes with some of them. He had a friend from whom he would buy a loaf stuffed with taamiya and carry it off tucked under his arm, and another friend from whom he bought the cheapest kind of cigarettes, which he kept in a metal tin above his belt, between his naked body and his outer garment. Then he would leave his friends for the sidewalk outside the mosque where—as he put it—he would enjoy a breath of fresh air and meet the newcomers of the day. When the novelty had worn off he would return to his place, seat himself, mutter a grace, and eat his meal. On finishing it, he would kiss the palm and back of his hand in gratitude, give thanks to God, and, settling his body into a relaxed position, light up a cigarette and smoke it with great gusto, for he was a man who took his pleasures seriously. Then he would disappear from the square and not return until just before sunset, when he would lay out the evening basket. As for his supper, it consisted of a loaf of bread and a piece of halva that he would buy from his neighbor whose shop lay north of his pitch; after which he would vanish from the square as it emptied of passersby. I don't know where he slept, though I did hear that he shared a mat with a toothless, bedridden hag in a small room under the curve of some steps at the farthermost end of a steep lane.

Had he ever married? Did he have any children or rela-
tives? I don't know. Because of my liking for Abu Khalil I
have no wish to talk here of the things I have heard about
his strange relationship with that bedridden, evil-smelling
old woman—Ibrahim has a kindly heart—nor do I want to
talk about the way he was unfaithful to her from time to
time, when God provided him with the necessary money
and vigor, on a hill close by Sayyida, for there is nothing I
am more reluctant to do than speak evil of this holy quarter
and its inhabitants.

One clear, radiant day Abu Khalil arrived at his customary
place on the sidewalk to find the far corner occupied by a
woman surrounded by three young children, with a fourth
at her breast, its eyes closed in swooning ecstasy as though it
were imbibing wine. The catastrophic thing about this was
that she was sitting in front of a basket filled with radishes,
rocket, and leeks, and when she began calling out, "Sun-
kissed radishes, a millieme the bundle!" her piercing voice
rang out through the whole square. O Provider, O
Omniscient! For a while Abu Khalil sat watching her in
silence, then he sighed and took himself a little way off. He,
too, began to call his wares, trying to raise his voice above
hers, but unable to do so he broke into a fit of coughing. He
wanted to speak to her, to ask her where she came from and
why she had chosen this particular place, but she paid no
attention to him. With one hand she sold her wares, with
the other she managed her children, transferring the
drugged infant with a mere bend of her knee from one
breast to the other, and then moving toward her water-cool-
er like a cripple, so that a little of her thigh showed naked.
But this had no effect—Abu Khalil's heart was so incensed
against her that he was not in an amorous mood. No doubt,

he assured himself, this was but a fleeting intrusion, and everything would be all right the next day.

But the following morning he found her there before him as large as life. He began turning his gaze toward her, toward the passers-by and his neighbors, getting up and sitting down again, leaving his basket and going off to tell his friends this depressing piece of news. Then he would return only to find her voice ringing through the square as though calling together her kin on the fateful Day of Resurrection.

During these days Abu Khalil bought five cigarettes instead of his usual ten.

He was at his wit's end and sought to dispel his anxiety by watching this brazen woman who had trespassed on his pitch and was competing with him in the earning of his daily bread. The strange thing was that he started to become interested in her and tried to exchange smiles with her on one occasion. Days went by and his basket crept closer to Badr's; it was as though he wanted to say to her, "Come, let's go into partnership together"; but he didn't do it.

Badr felt that she was firmly established and that Ibrahim was powerless against her; she realized that she had gained some sort of hold over him. So, one day, she deigned to reply to him and it was not long before she was bidding him keep an eye on the children when, at a call from nature, she had to go off to the plot of waste land close by the public fountain.

For a long time Abu Khalil neglected his own basket and gave up loafing around with his friends or standing at the door of the mosque, whether a breeze was blowing or not. A secret hope lay in his heart: perhaps Badr would prove to be his share of good fortune, rained down unexpectedly upon him by the heavens. Nothing would he love better than to hand over the leading-rein of his life to this resolute woman and to live under her protecting wing. She was a woman (although so much like a man) of whom he would have every reason to boast to all and sundry. He would ingratiate himself with her, would make her laugh so that he might laugh with her, and would wait until she first bit off a mouthful or two from the loaf before she passed it to him and he would eat from where her mouth had been, possibly receiving a taste of her spittle; it would be she who would wake him in the morning and cover him up at night; and when he behaved badly and stayed on with his friends and the shopkeepers, she would search him out and drag him back to where he ought to be. It was thus that he talked to himself. But would he ever broach the matter to her? He wouldn't dare, for he knew nothing about her, and there was no one in the square who knew her.

At this time Abu Khalil bought the taamiya for his lunch on credit.

One evening when his basket had drawn so close to hers that they were touching, Badr—without being asked—told him about her life. And thus it was that she too became one of the problems that it had been decreed should fall to Ibrahim's lot in this world. She told him that she was free yet not divorced, married yet living as a widow, for she had a husband of whose whereabouts she was ignorant, a man from Upper Egypt who used to carry a large bundle of vests, socks, and towels on his back, hawking them round the cafés. He would stay with her for a time and then suddenly disappear; on one occasion she had heard that he had gone to Lower Egypt, on another to the south, not knowing whether he was running away from her or from the fear of an old blood-feud, or whether he himself had a blood-feud which honor forced him to pursue. Almost a year and a half having passed since his last disappearance, she did not know whether he was dead or alive—though the odds were that he was alive and well, because the news of his death would have reached her, as he had his name and that of his village tattooed on his arm. Or had they perhaps skinned his body? Was he a murderer lingering in prison, or had he been murdered and was lying in some grave unknown to her? He had just disappeared, leaving her with her children. She had gone out in search of her daily bread, and chance had led her to a good man like Ibrahim Abu Khalil.

More days passed and they grew closer. Badr began to feel tenderly for Ibrahim and would buy him food without asking for money, for she had amalgamated their baskets, while both their earnings landed up in her pocket. She felt that her life had finally taken on this particular form. One day, accepting her position (and don't ask if it was from choice or necessity, it being no easy matter to find another Upper Egyptian to replace the absent man), she said to Ibrahim, "Your gallabiya is dirty. Come with me tonight and I'll wash it for you."

Abu Khalil was sitting in front of her, his back to the road. He began talking to her, oblivious of the passing of people and of time. Could he believe his eyes or were they playing him tricks? It seemed to him that her lips suddenly trembled, her teeth gleamed and her eyes, wide open, were sparkling. Her glance was glued to a spot behind him. He turned and found an Upper Egyptian, his back bowed under a large bundle, coming toward them with measured gait. It needed but one glance to tell him that this was a hard and merciless man, one who could not be trifled with. The man lowered his burden, squatted down, and wiped away the sweat from him brow.

"How are you?" was all he had to say to Badr.

"Everything is well," she answered. "Thank God for your safe return!"

The young Upper Egyptian was silent for a while. Then, turning his head, he directed but one glance at Abu Khalil. Reassured, he turned to his wife and said:

"Everything comes to pass in time, but patience is good."

Poor Ibrahim rose, shaking the dust from his backside, and disappeared from their sight, swallowed up by the crowds in the square.

Many days passed, during which I didn't see him. Some say that he was taken ill with fever, others that the old bedridden woman had learned about Badr and had put something—for which she had had to wait until nature took its monthly course with a woman younger than herself—into his food, and that this had caused him grievous harm.

For a long time I was absent from the square and its inhabitants. When I returned and passed by the sidewalk facing the Turk who sold halva, I found neither Badr of the many offspring nor Ibrahim.

Then one day it chanced that I went out early on some business or other and entered the square before the shops had opened. My teeth were chattering with the cold, for we were then in the Coptic month of Tuba, which is proverbially the peak of winter. Barefooted beings thrust their swollen fingers under their armpits and walked as though treading on thorns; from time to time a harsh, raucous cough rang through the square, followed by silence; then muttered scraps of conversation could be clearly heard from voices still heavy with sleep and phlegm. In spite of all the people to be seen coming and going, one could not help having the sensation of being in a deserted city, which nei-

ther knew nor was known by those passers-by. Suddenly I
bumped into Ibrahim Abu Khalil: his clothes were tattered
and torn, his head and feet bare, his walk a sort of totter,
though his somber manner of looking at one was the same
as ever, and his smile unchanged.

He had gone out at this early hour to do his job, which
had to be finished before traffic unfolded in the square. He
had a new occupation, providing incense—a job requiring
no more than a pair of old scales, a thick chain, some saw-
dust, and a few bits of frankincense and wormwood. These,
together with chunks of bread, he would put into a nosebag
slung around his shoulder, into which some millieme and
half-millieme pieces had perhaps also been thrown.

The moment I saw him I realized that this was the occupation to which Abu Khalil had been born. I should have
expected him to have ended up in it, for it suited his temperament admirably, being an easy job that provides its
practitioners with the pleasures of loafing about and coming
across all kinds and descriptions of people. Besides which,
the earnings were steady—being in the form of subscrip-
tions—and there was no fixed price. He was his own master
and there was no fear of his goods spoiling if business was
bad. While a man in such an occupation would admit that
he does not attain the status of those peddlers who gain their
livelihood with the sweat of their brow, he cannot on the
other hand be accused of mendicancy, for there he is in front
of you, going off to work with the tools of his trade in his
hand.

If this was how his occupation was regarded by the major-
ity of those practicing it, it was something altogether different in Abu Khalil's view. He had tired of trade in its various
forms, having found it to be a tug-of-war of deceit, calcula-

tion, and endless haggling over milliemes. The incense business, however, was based solely on emotion, and he was confident that his greeting, with which shopkeepers would begin their day, was bound to be auspicious, emanating from a heart that was pure, devout, and affectionate. Poor Abu Khalil! He understood neither life nor the nature of human beings.

For many days after this I was often in his company, and saw with my own eyes Master Hassàn the barber (who was no simpleton!) unwilling to pay him his millieme until he had dragged him into the shop to fumigate the chair, the mirror, and the small brass basin with its edge cut away to allow for the customer's neck; I also saw the owner of the National Restaurant pick him out a single taamiya left over from yesterday or the day before; as for the Turk, he would give him a millieme, irritated and resentful, and send him packing. When most of the shopkeepers had got used to him, they would give him the millieme whether there was any incense floating upward or not, and so Abu Khalil became negligent about his business, and his coals were dead for the greater part of the morning; or, if there was a faint glow, all that issued forth was an evil-smelling black smoke repellent to the nostrils.

One clear, radiant day I was walking beside Ibrahim when I felt a sudden hush descend on the square, just as the weather grows calm before the advent of a cyclone and the eye imagines that the sky is quivering like a bat's wing. Then a man with hawk-like eyes approached from Marasina Street, wearing a garment made up of seventy patches, a green turban on his head, and with a brisk, determined, indefatigable gait; his body erect, his tongue unceasingly chanting prayers and supplications, holding a brazier from which rose beautifully fragrant smoke, the brazier's chain sparkling yellow. O Provider, O Omniscient!

On the first day the shopkeepers sharply repulsed this newcomer, for they were Abu Khalil's customers and it wasn't reasonable to buy two blessings, one of which might spoil the other, on the same morning. But when he returned on the second, the third, and the fourth day, he received his first milliemes. Then he did the rounds of all the shops once again, whether the owner had taken pity on him or not. I was fascinated by this man's perseverance and strength of purpose. Leaving my bleary-eyed friend, I went off after this extraordinary newcomer and found myself being dragged along at a brisk pace from Sayyida Zaynab to Bab al-Khalq Square, to the Citadel and thence to Sayyida Aisha and across the Cemetery to Sayyida Nafisa and so to Suyufiya and Khayyamiya and Mitwalli Gate. Then he went to a small café in Sayyidna al-Hussein, where he took off his green turban and sat down to smoke a narghile. Breathless and dripping with sweat, I sat down beside him, having seen how he had walked for a whole hour to get one customer. Never in my life have I met anyone who strove to earn his living with the perseverance, patience, and energy of that man.

Poor Ibrahim left his brazier and began to content himself with passing by the shopkeepers empty-handed, in the hope that they would remember him and dispense their usual charity. His income decreased and he was sometimes forced to stand in the middle of the square, or at the Sayyida Zaynab Gate, so that some visitors might press their charity into his hand, taking him for a beggar too shy to ask for alms. The strange thing was that after a while Abu Khalil worked up a clientele of a few faithful customers who would search him out to give him what they could. Poor Abu

Khalil! He understood neither life nor the nature of human beings.

One clear, radiant day as poor Ibrahim sat in his accustomed place, a loud shout rang out close by him, which echoed through the whole square: "The Ever-living! The Eternal!" People gathered around a man who had fallen down in a trance, seized by religious ecstasy. A woman, dressed in a black gown, yellow mules, and a necklace of large amber beads, stood at his head and broke out into trilling cries. The stricken man came to, but his mouth was closed and he uttered not a word; his squinting eyes, darkened with kohl, stared round at the faces of those gathered about him and filled with tears. Then he raised his hands, loaded with blue, green, and red rings, wiped his face, and prepared to gather up the money.

When Abu Khalil heard that very same scream at the very same hour on the second and third days, he left his place and turned toward the mosque, mumbling, "O Mother of the Destitute! Give me succor!"

He had tired of life; illness and weakness held him in their grip. The film on his eyes had grown worse, and his back was bowed. With heavy steps he moved toward the shrine of Sayyida Zaynab, granddaughter of the Prophet and Mother of the Destitute; around it were ranks of squatting beggars—it seemed as though they had been created like that, their backs propped against its wall, making a circle like lice around a poor man's collar. Little hope for him to find himself a place in the 'first class' by the door! So he left and went around the mosque until he came to the place of ablution, where he sat himself down by its door. Those who had come before him and had seniority turned and gave him a withering look: nobody hates a beggar like a beggar.

Here I left Abu Khalil and dissociated myself from him, for he had joined the people of a world that is not our world. He was in a world from which there was no exit; it had but one entrance and above it was written: "The Gate of Farewell."

A Story
from Prison

@

The fact that it was a duty many times repeated did away
with any feelings the sergeant might have had as he shoved
those under arrest into the cell. But with this particular man
he was annoyed; with his mouth screwed up and his grip
cruelly tight, he enjoyed cursing him and striking him on
the back of the neck. It was not because his eyes had alighted on legs that were sore and chapped, or that his nose was
assailed by a disgusting smell emanating from a dirty blue
gallabiya patched in numerous places with pieces of darker
colors, for he was accustomed to such things in the peasants
who crossed his path. Rather, it was because, ever since
learning that the accused was one of the band of gypsies the
police had been after, he had regarded him with an eye of
repugnance. It was not the look one man gives to another,
but the scrutiny accorded by a superior species to an inferi-
or one. His hand had no sooner fallen on the other man's

shoulder than he was seized with a feeling of disgust that was close to nausea. Gypsies! Were they human beings?

The gypsy entered the cell with a smile on his mouth brought about by embarrassment, a smile that was cold and doltish and became wider and more idiotic when his gaze alighted on a young man sitting in a corner, who he saw was also smiling. Turning his face away and squatting down in another corner, he proceeded to ruminate and so pass the time. His inactivity did not last long. After a while he again glanced furtively at the young man, gradually arousing in the latter a desire to enter into conversation. He began by asking the young man his name, what village he came from and what he was charged with, and from there the conversation branched out. The name of a famous criminal came up and he mentioned that he knew him, that they were in fact distantly related.

"You're both from the same village?" the young man asked.

"Yes, he and I are from one and the same part of the village."

"I heard the policeman calling you a gypsy. How was it you got mixed up with the gypsies, then, if you're a peasant?"

The noise in the police station courtyard grew louder as the sound of rifles being put into racks was heard, with here and there the crash of policemen's boots. A three-sentry patrol came along and sat down to chat alongside the prison cell. Their words reached the two men clearly, as well as their bursts of laughter. The gypsy drew closer to the young man until he was sitting beside him—he had not been friendly with a peasant for a long time. In the dreariness of prison and amid the unusual hubbub, there was kindled in his heart a sympathy and affection for his companion. It may have been as a result of all these circumstances that he began to talk, neither evasively nor aggressively. He was not so much recounting his story as reliving his past.

"I had rented fourteen qirats of land—just over half an acre—from the umda's brother, and I had a few head of sheep that I let loose in the fields in spring. When the Nile flood came I had no work, so the fellow with the land said to me: 'Ellewi, seeing as you've nothing to do, why don't you go up to Minya with my sheep and take them to a merchant I know there. I can assure you, my friend, I'll make it worth your while.' I said to him: 'The journey's too difficult for me.' He replied: 'You're experienced with sheep, and I've chosen you—you're my man. The journey isn't as difficult as you think. Just keep along the Ibrahimiya Canal, going northward all the way, and you'll find yourself at Minya.' And the man went off, bought me a fine knife, gave me a donkey, and handed over sixty-five head of sheep. I went out of the village with them, with the floodwater lying a foot high on the fields, and continued driving the sheep ahead of me along the embankment of the Ibrahimiya Canal."

Sheep, though not timid animals, are not easily driven. They move slowly, and if not continually urged on, come to a stop, and only a vigilant stick will bring them together once they get scattered. Sometimes Ellewi would have to gather them together with his long cudgel to allow passage to approaching cars, while at other times he would have to descend into the fields behind some stray ram. The whole day might well pass without him uttering more than a drawn-out, whistled, shushing sound. With his long cudgel he would give sharp taps to the sheep's backs to bring them together into a single, easily managed flock, while their short, delicate feet stirred up clouds of dust. Their cries of *ma . . . ma . . .* were continuous, some short and staccato, others almost a form of speech, in which there was an unmistakable call for help. Some calls were harsh and husky, issuing from throats that had desiccated with the years, whereas others were like the twanging of the thin string of a musical instrument and emanated from small lambs, full of vivacity and exuberance, whose bellies were not yet distinguishable from their backs and whose mode of progression was by sideways leaps and playful buttings. A flock of sheep also bears within its fold the chain that binds life with death.

Ellewi, fearing that a young lamb would lose its way, raised it up by its legs, at which it set up a loud, continuous bleating. He walked along with it, cleaving a way amid the sheep, every now and again lowering his hand so that it fell on a wave of wool set ablaze by the sun; the collected dust, mixed with the animals' sweat, had become hot and sticky above scalding bodies that bore their suffering with patience. When he reached the donkey, he opened a bag and placed the lamb inside. A skinny ewe, cleaving its way with an effort even greater than his own, had followed after him with a will that spoke of its determination not to be diverted by anything, and which replied to each *ma* with an answer containing a tenderness that expressed the loving concern of a mother.

Ellewi's appearance gave no indication that he was capable of bearing the burden of looking after a flock of sheep, for he was in his early youth. While one's eyes might not notice the signs of his pharaonic ancestry—his tall stature and broad chest—they would not miss his obvious thinness and the lack of proportion between his large, splayed feet and his spindly legs. Under his collarbone was a hollow, possibly the result of hunger; the exposed hair of his chest ended at the two protruding bones. His face consisted of taut skin and muscle; whatever happened, no spare flesh quivered there. When he moved his jaw, the surface of his temple was broken up into hollows and bumps. He was nevertheless ever on the go, his energy renewed by some mysterious power that flowed in the Valley and was no less forceful than the Nile itself, a power that had not been crushed by the building of a pagan monument like the Pyramids or by being entombed by the passage of thousands of years.

Ellewi would cover great distances with nothing remaining in his mind of the journey other than the names of the villages or the small, white memorial domes set up to various holy men; some of these would lie high up on the canal embankment so that the village could bury its dead around them, while others would be down in the agricultural land flooded by the Nile so that the crops might benefit from their blessing. Ellewi, like the peasant he was, and because he was making the journey for the first time, had little contact with the places he passed, nothing attracting his attention unless it affected him personally. Thus he was not at all impressed by the Ibrahimiya Canal embankment, which looked ugly under the burning sun of Upper Egypt, screened by a thick cloud of dirt stretching out before him like a vast ribbon of piled-up, jagged-edged earth; continually rising and falling, its uneven surface was ever changing its mind as to whether to be narrow or broad. It was rendered even uglier by the fact that it was much higher than the canal itself, so that nothing could be seen of the trees planted at the water's edge except for short branches that blocked the view, branches that the person walking along the embankment could touch with his hand. What would Ellewi say if someone were to tell him that much of the height of the embankment was not made up of earth, that deep within it there were also many skeletons of peasants, among them perhaps some of his own forebears, who had dug the canal across four provinces with their primitive picks, perhaps even with their nails? When a peasant died, the earth was piled on top of him, just as he was, with his basket, his pick, and his one blue gallabiya. The canal had eaten up their bodies, wiping away their flesh and the lash marks on their skin.

"On the fourth day, just after the call to afternoon prayer, I reached Nazali Ganub. I was intending to walk straight on and spend the night with the sheep in Sanabu, but I don't know what it was that made me bring the sheep to a halt in front of this village. I'd be lying if I said I was tired—perhaps it was because I'd found a derelict mill on the embankment."

The young man interrupted him in an almost sarcastic tone, like a man listening to a child. "Or was it just your destiny that it happened like that?"

The young man was still smiling. His eyes never left Ellewi, whom he regarded as an entertaining spectacle, for since feeling that Ellewi was treating him like a brother he had despised him. Whenever he interrupted the other's conversation with his mocking remarks—which was often—his body shook with pleasure.

"The Lord knows best. I didn't believe it when I found the mill had a big wall, so I got the sheep arranged and said to myself: 'You're going to have a good night's sleep tonight, with no sheep escaping and you having to run around after them.' So I settled myself down. When the time for evening prayer came, I moved close to the sheep, took off my gallabiya, and put my head on my arm to sleep. But my eyes hadn't yet met up with sleep when I found a group of people making their way toward me from the direction of the village. In their midst were a couple of donkeys, and some goats were going in front of them. When they came to where I was, I realized they were a band of gypsies. I said to myself: "What rotten bad luck—but maybe, my boy, they'll go straight on." I got up and hid myself to see what would happen. They came right alongside me and stopped, and after a while I found them spreading their things out around me."

Two men went to the donkeys and unloaded some thin screens, which they leaned up against each other—and there, in front of Ellewi, were two small tents. They knocked some pegs into the ground, to which they tied their goats. A woman took out a cooking-pot and sat down to rub it clean with earth, then went to the canal. One of them brought out three pieces of stick tied up in a bundle. He unfolded them, fixing their feet in the ground, and brought a kettle, which he hung in the middle, lighting a fire beneath it and leaning his head forward and blowing at it. After a while there was the smell of tea, and the gypsies became aware of their neighbor.

"One of them said to me: 'Please have a drink of tea with us.' So I got up and went over to them and sat down."

"Had it been a long time since you'd had a drink of tea?" the young man asked him.

"You know that peasants are stupid and won't say 'No' to any invitation. But to tell you the truth, I was frightened, what with all those stories in our village about gypsies being thieves and kidnappers and playing tricks you'd never even think of. I said to myself: 'My boy, keep an eye on these people.' They had a girl with them, who went back and forth in front of me. I only noticed her when I saw the men frowning at her. Not one of them would speak to her in a decent, friendly way, all the time shouting and snapping at her.

Sometimes she'd make a reply and sometimes she'd just walk by in silence. I don't know what she'd done to them for them to swear at her without listening to what she had to say, saying such things as: 'You crazy girl, you'll see. We'll show you!' After that, every time she passed in front of me I took a good look at her."

He saw she had a dark brown face, almost completely round, and a thin nose; she had a green dot on her forehead, and a recent tattoo on her chin. She was short and straight-backed, and the way she was constantly moving her head showed a very nervous disposition. She would hide her anger by visibly pressing down on her lips, which made them longer and more pinched. When she came to pass round the glasses, a smell that was alien to his nose was wafted from her to him, a mixture of sweat and dirt and a perfume containing cloves and sandalwood. Before he knew it Ellewi was engaged in conversation with them.

"We went on talking and they went on asking me about the sheep: Where was I taking them? How many had I got? I was frightened they were distracting me because of some plot they were hatching. I said to myself: 'Get up and look to your sheep.' I went back to my place but wasn't able to sleep at first. Then no sooner had my eyes closed, well after midnight, than I was woken by the barking of a dog and found that my sheep were all rushing about in front of three policemen, whose horses' eyes gleamed like sparks in the darkness—I can still recall them even now! I went crazy, running about and falling over. Every time I turned in the direction of the gypsies I saw the policemen knocking down the tents. The fire was out and turned to smoke. I heard them being cursed: 'Thieves! Robbers! Sons of bitches!' Their arms were waving above their heads as they screamed:

'Have mercy, Sergeant.' But it was no good. They rounded them up on a chain, and I went on collecting the sheep until, thanks be to the Lord, I got them all together. I went back to my place and was about to take off my gallabiya and go to sleep when I looked out and found the gypsy girl rolled up in a heap right up against the wall. To tell you the truth, I was trembling from the shock of it. What a business! What sort of mess was I getting into?

"'Hey girl, what are you up to? What brought you here?'

She motioned to me with her finger. Then, when the police had quite taken themselves off, she flung herself at me and said, 'I'm at your mercy.' She told me, 'Those men wanted to kill me. They thought I gave them away in the Qusiya robbery. They put us all in prison, and as soon as they came out they stole again. I beseech you to take me with you. I'll go wherever you go, just so long as I get away from those people.'"

The gypsy girl stretched out her arms and clasped him round the neck. She was neither trembling nor breathing quickly—the only thing that had changed in her was that the tightness of her lips had disappeared and they now looked swollen and revealed two large teeth. She lowered her eyes. Was it that he was tired, or was it because it was Ellewi's first experience? Perhaps, too, it was because he had never before smelled at close quarters the scent of cloves and sandalwood. Whatever the reason, Ellewi felt his strength melt away between her hands as his arms dropped limply to his side. There came back to his mind the image of this woman passing in front of him as he sat drinking tea with her companions and he remembered the way she had of tossing her head. He had not realized then—though he did now—that these tossings of the head held an extraordinary attraction for him, a powerful fascination. His silence lasted a long time, and he analyzed it as being an effect of his upbringing, which had taught him since he was a boy to stand in awe of gypsies. But he did not repel the woman's arms; in fact after a while he had the sensation that the numbness in his nerves had been replaced by a throbbing in his forehead, a dryness in his throat, and a trembling in his heart. All these things combined to fill his veins with blood that boiled and thundered in his ears. Then his arms were on hers and he was further inflamed when she drew gradually closer to him, impelled toward him by a feeling that was a mixture of joy and defiance. Perhaps her passion was not for the man but resulted from savoring the pleasure of her freedom on this her first night. No sooner had the man returned her embrace than there burst forth from its hiding place a strong desire that had long been suppressed, and in its unloosing a tornado was set free. It was none the less careful not to expend itself too quickly, curbing its impetuosity and veiling its vehemence with a screen of deliberation and poise. Her whole concern was to give the man what he had not previously had, and to take from him as much as she could. As his mouth lay on hers there shone in her eyes—despite the darkness—the image of conquest. Were instinct to have had a body and were it to have looked down upon them, it would have nodded its head in pride and satisfaction, and it would have excused itself for this by saying that while it was not happy about the bashful and timid manner in which most people indulge their instinct, there were, here and there, at different times, a few individuals who realized its full potential, persons who gave up their very souls to it and allowed themselves to be wholly possessed. The kiss did not last long, for the woman came to her senses and became aware of where she was. She therefore rose to her feet and, drawing the man by the hand, entered through a gap in the wall of the mill, where the darkness wrapped them round. This night it was for the dog to guard both the sheep and its master.

"To cut a long story short, she spent the night with me. I said to her, 'My good girl, I'm a God-fearing man and I want to have the blessing of the law.' She said, 'I have given myself to you.' I said to her, 'I accept, and if anyone hears about this I'll say that many peasants marry in country places purely by mutual consent.'"

"But not on the embankment, they don't," said his friend, "—and not with gypsies!"

"At the time I didn't know what I was doing."

He did not know how he had got any sleep as he drove the flock along. When day had come he had found himself not the master of a flock but the slave of a fate whose staff made no distinction in the way it drove both humans and sheep. Despite this, he felt that this woman had bestowed upon him a pleasure that was new to him: like a tired man he had been led to her, finding after his exertions a comfortable bed. Ellewi let himself relax and rely upon her, not caring, in this honeyed state of lethargy, what fetters she bound him with, so long as the stream of vitality that had been awakened in him—and that thereafter he was unable to curb—found no other outlet but her in which to swell and pour forth. Ellewi forgot the days of his past and confined his attention to the moment he was in, and in the morning he walked off, still in a state of bewilderment, behind his flock.

"We went off at dawn, with me in a daze. We made Dayrut—no, no, I'm forgetting. After we'd been walking a while I looked round for the dog and didn't find it. I went back to look for it and found it near a tree in the throes of death."

The dog was lying with its hindquarters flat on the ground, its head raised on quivering forepaws, its body shaken with convulsions. The dog stared at its master, and in its eyes there shone a momentary gleam of hope, which was quickly extinguished by a deep and silent sadness. He had never before seen eyes weeping like the glassy, staring eyes of the dog, addressing him and saying, "Will this be the last time you'll see me?" It opened its mouth, but death placed his hand over it and the dog was unable to bark. Instead of a yelp came streams of viscid slaver that told of the unknown pain that boiled in the animal's stomach. Ellewi did not understand the reason for what had happened. Perhaps someone had beaten it, for many was the peasant who cruelly beat stray dogs, or perhaps some young boy had thrown a stone at it—this vicious act that the first criminal tendency in a child's head puts into practice. He stretched out his hand to run it across the dog's back and found it undamaged. He felt the gypsy girl by his side.

"She had come to sit beside me and watch. I looked at her and she said to me, 'My people have poisoned it—they wanted to steal your sheep while you were asleep. They weren't given the time, the Devil take them. Don't be angry, tomorrow you'll find another one. And just so you'll feel better I've brought you two of their goats—there in the middle.' I said to her, 'Are they yours, the two goats?' She said, "No, they're theirs."'"

The young man again interrupted him. "Got yourself a bit of loot for free."

"By Allah, I wasn't happy about taking them but what could I do?"

Just as his dog, lying between the hands of death, had been unable to bark, so he, between the hands of the woman who had stolen his mind, was unable to open his mouth. Nothing was more expressive of the difference between their two natures than the slight smile that played on the gypsy girl's mouth, matched by a perceptible frown on the peasant's brow.

The dog's trembling grew less, little by little, until its movements ceased altogether and the flies dared to settle on its mouth and eyes. As Ellewi rose to return to his flock, grief for the dog he was leaving behind contended within him with a feeling of dread at the two goats that walked in front of him and that embodied the first crime he had ever committed; he who had lived all his years in awe of the police station, who shook before the umda and would greet policemen with respect.

"From the first day I found that the gypsy girl was clever. She would save the milk she drew off and sell it. In the past I hadn't known what to do with it. Also she weaned several lambs for me, having fixed a bag on each of the ewes. I had forgotten about the two goats. I said to myself: 'Tomorrow, my lad, you'll return to your village and you'll raise your own sheep, and if you've got yourself a girl as clever as this one, why not take in other people's sheep and keep them with you and graze them? Tomorrow, my lad, you'll have yourself a better living—your Lord is generous.'

"After several days I reached Mallawi and found some bare land at the entrance to the town. I left the sheep there and went up to the embankment in front of a café and sat down. The girl disappeared below with the sheep. Right from the beginning the night was cursed. I don't know what came over the girl— she had turned completely against me by the morning."

The gypsy girl had gone down to walk slowly among the ewes. There was nothing to keep her with the flock, likewise nothing to prompt her to return to Ellewi.

She had begun to be bored with her new regulated life, which proceeded along a known course, and she yearned again for her old nomadic existence. Her whole pleasure lay in being hounded from one village to another, her link with each place not exceeding a single night. The initial passion had waned and there was now nothing more to Ellewi than a peaceful man whose goodness she could be sure of, and she felt nostalgia for a life that was half love and half hostility. The gypsies are egoists and do not accept strangers in their midst. She had continued to submit to one of their men, not from love but through necessity, and she used to find her pleasure in the continual struggle between her passionate nature and her bitter dislike of him. What greater pleasure was there than refusing to submit until after a flood of desire had risen up to her mouth, almost drowning her and making her forget her dislike, great though it might be? Whenever fulfillment coincides with breaking point the spirit enjoys the most sublime extremes of ecstasy. For the present she submitted, be the flood at her feet or at her knees; she did not know the pleasure of satiety because she had been deprived of the pleasure of being hungry. While she did not hate Ellewi, she would have liked him to have been a gypsy.

The light of a lamp that lit up the embankment where Ellewi was sitting cut through the gypsy girl's thoughts. A café came into view; in the center, under a lamp, was a wooden dais, where a man sat with a two-stringed fiddle, singing. She forgot her thoughts and came up to listen to the story of how Marei, Yahya, and Yunis were imprisoned at the palace of Zanati in Tunis, and the return of Prince Abu Zeid to the ruins. The man let out a succession of shouts at which the murmurings of those seated abated and all gave ear to the story and the poetry. As the night drew on, the breathing of the lamp grew more constricted, choked by a thick circle of mosquitoes that, despite the rising smoke, had congealed like dirt around it. The universe was wrapped in total silence; the sky in its darkness was as though the wing of a bat had alighted on the earth. From time to time it gave a slight shudder, the result of the vibration of those few stars that flicker and then grow still. Neither the lamp with its hissing, nor the singer with his fiddle, was able to disperse any of the sadness that oppressed the universe. Was night the corpse of day and this sadness the hymn of death? Or was the world in mourning because it sensed it was perishing little by little? Or perhaps it was as a result of the thousands of oriental souls created by God sad and sore of heart that wander about this vast expanse? This very same sky, when covering the north, is perhaps the epitome of joy, fulfillment, and ecstasy, and the flickering of its stars a dance.

This atmosphere weighed heavily upon the fiddle, which gave out a monotonously plaintive sound. The whole world stood on one side, the fiddle on the other, and a dialogue took place between them, each giving up its secrets to the other. So affected by the story were the listeners that the singer disappeared from their view and Abu Zeid took shape before them, sitting on the dais and letting out his warlike cries. Times became so mixed up in their minds that they did not know whether it was he who had been brought back to life to recount to them the stories of his battles, or they who had been transported by some magic hand to his dis-

tant age. The poet chose an ode he knew from experience
would make an impression on his audience, and he ended
his evening with it. The last verses he sang were:

O woe, my heart, at what happened
When with six fetters separation shackled me.
Outwitted by the worries that came to me,
When will those old days return?
Destiny's voice answered by saying:
Time that has passed will ne'er again return.
Weep, O eye, for the time that has passed,
Your recompense is from God the One, the Adored.

Did the anonymous poet know, as he described the suffer-
ings of his heroes, that his poetry would be heard by this
gypsy girl on the embankment and that she would receive it
like a knife-thrust? Perhaps he knew this and more than this,
or otherwise how was it that he pronounced what was in her
innermost being as though he already knew her, had been
associated with her, and had heard her grievance many
times? Her eyes watered with copious tears, then her stubbornness and unruliness awoke and she suppressed her worries. She rose to go to sleep, having resolved to act on the
idea that had been occupying her mind those last few days.

"I woke up and found her walking along the embankment, her gallabiya hitched up under her arm. She was walking slowly but I realized immediately that she was running
away from me. I went after her, caught up with her, and
seized her by the arm.

"'Where are you going?'

"'Walking . . . .'

"'Where to?'

"'Off west, to the desert—maybe I'll be able to join my people there.'

"'By yourself?'

"'Yes. Let me go my way and you yours.'

"'My dear girl, I've told you, the sheep aren't mine, their owner is in Minya, which is now no more than a stone's throw from us, after which I'm going straight back to the village with you."

"'Your village and all that's in it can go to hell,' she told me right out."

The young man stared at Ellewi as though expecting the angry outburst of a peasant who accepts everything but the insulting of his kinsfolk. However, Ellewi had been almost completely separated from his family and kinsfolk by that time; the insult did not arouse his sensitivity, and he swallowed it.

"I said to her, 'Let's not go to the village. All right, we'll go anywhere you want.'

"'Come with me.'

"'And the sheep?'

"'Bring them with you.'

"'They're not mine.'

"As though annoyed at what I'd said she sharply averted her face. She walked off again and was nearly out of sight. While all this was happening, the Devil was trying to turn my head."

Ellewi stood there, every vein in him pulsating and alert. Her impetuosity had intoxicated him, had made him lose his head. He cast a glance at the woman, then a glance at the flock of sheep, while the Devil stood in front of him, smiling and holding the balance. The scale came down on the side of the woman.

"'Slow up,' I shouted at her. 'Slow up, I'm coming.'

"I ran to the sheep and drove them from the embankment to another road leading west to the desert, and we walked off without giving the world a thought. I really didn't know where it was all going to end.

"That night I saw her do something extraordinary. We were passing by a farm and saw a hen pecking about in the road. The girl took a long piece of thread out from her pocket with a grain of maize tied on the end. She threw it in front of the hen, which picked it up. It stuck in its throat and the hen began scraping its beak on the ground. It wanted to cry out but couldn't. The girl pulled the hen toward her very gradually and put it under her arm. As soon as we'd put a distance between ourselves and the village she slaughtered it. We got to the desert . . ."

"Wait a bit—who ate the chicken?"

"We ate it together."

"Why was it the girl didn't pull this trick before?"

"How should I know? This food was like poison to me and I prayed to Allah for His protection."

"You're right there—someone who steals sixty-five head of sheep chokes on a chicken!"

Ellewi was silent and sighed loud and long. The moon had disappeared and the glow from a lamp hanging some way off reached the solitary prison cell in the middle of the station courtyard. The loud thumping of horses' hooves on the asphalt rang out and a donkey brayed alongside them. Then the place quietened down again and Ellewi, with broken heart, returned to his story. His affection for his companion had waned, preoccupied as he was with himself as he recounted his adventures in brief: he was not reliving his past so much as remembering with an effort some of what had happened to him.

"In the desert we met up with her group of people. She was alone with their leader for a while. God knows what they were saying about me. I saw her pointing at the sheep and the man looking at them as though he were counting them. I went off with the sheep. Two or three days later I found that one of them had gone missing. I must say my blood really boiled. I got hold of the girl and said to her: 'If someone doesn't want to lose his life he'd better not go near the sheep.'

"'We're now gypsies together,' she said. 'All our belongings are together.' I said to her, 'Gypsies or not, I don't hold with such talk.' She screwed her mouth up at me and stopped talking to me. After a couple of days I went to her and said, "My good girl, I've sold my people and my honor for you.' Though she made it up with me, she was really having me on. Every other moment she would say to me: 'Don't be afraid for your sheep, gypsies don't steal from one another.' Even so, every time we came near a market I'd find one or two head of sheep missing. She had lied to me."

"She hadn't lied to you. It was you who'd considered yourself a gypsy, while they didn't consider you one. That's why they were stealing from you. You were booty for them, fair game."

"The sheep ended up at ten, then five. I said to myself, 'What's it all about, lad? Are you going to be left stark naked, or what?' One night I fooled them and got up before dawn and drove away those that were left and went to the market, where I sold them once and for all."

"You fooled them? After all, weren't the sheep yours?"

Ellewi did not reply but continued with his story.

"About a week ago they bundled me off with them and they stole—we stole together—a sack of cotton from a field. Last night we were arrested."

It was inevitable that Ellewi should taste some of the insults and harassment that gypsies experience. The night when the horsemen had attacked, the lashes had fallen, and the handcuffs had been fastened, had come and gone. However, spending time in the company of gypsies had made him able to accept abuse, handcuffs, and the lash with equanimity. A year ago he had been a witness to what had befallen the gypsies, and his terror, as a spectator, had been greater than it was today as, after a beating, he walked in chains to the police station. In the year that had passed it was not so much his life that had been consumed as his morals and habits that had been demolished. He had been a peasant whose concern was with the Nile, the umda, the police station, and the boundaries of the land that he would measure by span of hand and length of finger. As for now, he was a gypsy concerned only with the day he was in: the whole world was before him and it had no boundaries. If he was able to get something from it, then he should grab it, and be happy.

"And the police brought her along with you?" the young man asked him.

"The girl? No, she got away again."

"Let's hope this time around she doesn't find someone else to bring down."

"No, where will she find anyone? As soon as I'm out I'll go off and start looking for her.'

This time the young man did not make fun of him. Yawning and stretching, he lay down on the ground. Before going to sleep he recited in a low voice, without singing it, this folk song:

Can you leave your beloved
Even if, O the pity, she's done you wrong

Or filled your glass with bitterness,
Stirred it round and given it you to drink?
No, not even if she's raised a stick against you
And, woe betide you, has driven you before her.
Night, O night, thus is my fate.

The Lamp
of Umm Hashim

My grandfather, Sheikh Ragab Abdullah, coming to Cairo as
a young boy with the men and women of the family to
obtain blessings from visiting the family of the Prophet,
would be pushed forward as they approached the entrance
to the Mosque of Sayyida Zaynab. The instinct to imitate
the others made it unnecessary to push the boy; along with
them, he would drop down and cover the marble doorstep
with kisses, while the feet of those going in and out of the
mosque almost knocked against his head. If their action was
witnessed by one of the self-righteous men of religion, he
would turn his face away in indignation at the times and
would invoke God's aid against idolatry, ignorance, and
such heresies. As for most people, they would simply smile
at the naivety of these country folk, with the smell of milk,
mud, and fenugreek emanating from their clothes; they
would understand in their hearts the warmth of these peo-

ple's longing and veneration for the place they were visiting, people unable to find any other way than this to express their emotions. Deeds, as the saying has it, are by intention.

As a young man, my grandfather moved to Cairo in search of work. It is no surprise that he should choose to live as near as possible to his much loved mosque. And so it was that he settled in an old house that was a religious endowment, facing the mosque's rear ablution basin in the alley named Ablution Lane. I say 'was' in the past tense because the heavy axe of the town-planning department has demolished it along with other Cairo landmarks. While the axe wrought its will, though, the soul of the square escaped unscathed, for the axe was able to wipe out and destroy only those things that were of brick and stone.

My grandfather later opened a store for grain in the square itself, and thus the family came to live within the precincts of Umm Hashim—Sayyida Zaynab—and under her protection: her holidays became our holidays, her feasts our feasts, and the mosque's muezzin the clock by which we told the time.

My grandfather enjoyed the blessings of Umm Hashim, and his business flourished. No sooner had his eldest son finished his studies at the elementary Qur'anic school than he took him into the business. As for the second son, he went to al-Azhar University, where he spent several unsuccessful years, after which he went back to our village to become its school teacher and the official responsible for performing marriages. There remained the youngest son, the last child—my uncle Ismail—for whom fate, and the improvement in his father's fortunes, made it possible to provide a brighter future. At first, his father was perhaps frightened, having forced his son to learn the Qur'an by

heart, to send him to al-Azhar, for he could see the young
boys in the square calling after young men with turbans:

Pull off the turban—

Under the turban a monkey you'll find!

But Sheikh Ragab, with a heart full of hope, handed him
over to a government school, where he was helped by his
religious upbringing and village background, for he quickly
excelled by his good manners and his respect for his teach-
ers, together with deportment and much perseverance.
Though not elegantly dressed, his clothes were clean. More
than that, he was more manly and was capable of expressing
himself better than his pampered colleagues, the children of
town folk who were disadvantaged by faulty Arabic. It was-
n't long before he surpassed his fellows, and he had about
him a certain unmistakable bearing that caused the family's
hopes to be set on him.

While still a lad he came to be called Mr. Ismail or Ismail
Effendi and was treated like a grown man, being given the
best of food and fruits.

When he sat down to study, the father, while reciting his
prayers, would lower his voice to a whisper that was almost
a melting of tremulous devotion, while his mother walked
about on tiptoe, and even his orphan cousin Fatima al-
Nabawiya learned how to stop her chattering and to sit
silently in front of him like a slave-girl before her master.
She became accustomed to sit up with him into the night, as
though the lesson he was studying were hers, gazing at him
with her sore eyes with their inflamed lids, and with her
fingers ceaselessly at work on some piece of knitting. Who
was there to say to Ismail: Take note of those hands into
which has crept a strange life, a delicate touch, an awakened
sensitivity? Do you not realize that the sign of the approach

of blindness in a seeing person is when his hands begin to acquire sight?

"Get up and go to sleep, Fatima."

"It's still early—I'm not sleepy yet."

From time to time her eye would water and transform him into a blurred shape. Wiping her eye with the end of her sleeve, she would go back to gazing at him. For her, wisdom was to be found in every word he uttered.

Dear God! How was it possible for books to contain all those secrets and enigmas? How was it that the tongue could pronounce all those foreign languages? As he grew in stature in her eyes, the more she shrank and dwindled before him. His gaze might fall on her two pigtails and he would smile musingly. These girls! If only they knew how empty-headed they were!

When he retired to bed, and only then, did the family feel that its day had ended; only then did it begin to think about tomorrow's needs. Its life, its movements were dedicated to his comfort. A generation was annihilating itself so that a single member of its progeny might come into being: it was a love whose strength had attained the force of an animal instinct. The solicitous hen sits on her eggs, paralyzed and meek like a nun at prayer. Are such instincts a bountiful gift, or are they a tribute paid to some despotic tyrant of iron will, with a yoke around every neck, shackles on every leg? The family clung to this boy with the ardor of those deprived of all liberty and free will. Where in God's name was the beauty in it? The answer to that question lies in my heart. Whenever those past days were depicted to me, I would find my heart beating at the memory of them; there would appear before me the face of my grandfather, Sheikh Ragab, his face surrounded by a halo of pure light. As for my grandmother, the Lady Adeela, with her naive goodness, it would be stupid to think of her as being human, for, if so, then what would angels be like! How hateful and ugly the world would be were it to be devoid of such submission, such faith!

Year after year, Ismail came first in his class. When the results of the examination were announced, glasses of sherbet would be passed around the neighbors, even to the odd passerby. The woman selling taamiya and busara made from beans would make trilling cries of joy and would ask God to keep him safe, and Master Hassan, both barber and doctor for the district, would achieve his usual tip. The Lady Adeela, for her part, would burn incense, thus fulfilling her vows to Umm Hashim. Loaves of bread would be baked and stuffed with sprouting beans, and Umm Mohammed would carry them off in a basket on her head. No sooner did she appear in the square than the loaves would be seized, the basket would disappear, her milaya would be gone, and she would stumble bashfully back home, partly in amused anger at the greed of Sayyida's beggars. Her experience would provide the family with amusement for several days.

Thus, in the protection of God, then in that of Umm Hashim, Ismail grew up. His life did not take him outside the quarter itself and the square; the farthest excursion he ever made was to Manyal, where he would walk beside the river or stand on the bridge. With the coming of evening and the waning violence of the sun, when the sharp reflections and straight lines had changed to curves and illusions, the square would come to itself and would be empty of visitors and strangers. If you are of pure heart and conscience and listen carefully, you will be conscious of a deep, secret breathing traversing the square. Perhaps it is Sidi al-Itris, the mosque's doorkeeper—for is not his name numbered among the Servants?—sitting in his private quarters, shaking the dust of the day's work from his hands and clothing as he breathes a sigh of satisfaction. Were it your good fortune to hear this deep breathing, you might at that instant take a look at the dome and see it engirdled by a radiance of light, fading then growing stronger like the flickerings of a lamp toyed with by the breeze. This is the lamp of Umm Hashim that hangs over the shrine—walls cannot obscure its rays.

Slowly the square fills up again. Exhausted, sallow-faced, and bleary-eyed, each person is dressed in what chance has bestowed upon him, or, if you will, what he has found to hand. The calls of the street vendors make a mournful melody:

"Great green broad beans!"

"Eat something sweet and call down blessings on the Prophet!"

"Tender radishes!"

"Use a miswak for keeping your teeth clean, just as the Prophet did!"

What is the hidden tyranny they complain of! What is the burden that weighs down the breasts of them all! And yet, for all that, their faces show a kind of contentment and serenity. How easily they forget! Many are the hands that take in so few piasters and milliemes. Here there is no law, no standard measure, no fixed price; there is only custom, giving favors, and haggling, allowing the scales to tip freely and giving a fair weight, and sometimes being fraudulent and cheating. It's all free and easy. Rows of people are seated on the ground with their backs to the wall of the mosque; some squat on the pavement: a medley of men, women, and children. You don't know where they have come from nor how they will pass from sight: fruit that has fallen from the tree of life and has become moldy under its canopy.

Here is the school of beggars. One of them, his back weighed down under a sack full of bits of bread, calls out:

"A crust of bread for God's sake. O doers of good—I'm hungry."

Then there's the young girl who springs up all of a sudden in the middle of the lane, naked, or almost so:

"O you who clothe a woman, O Muslim—may God never bring such a scandal to a woman of yours!"

Her screeching voice attracts faces to the windows. Her bewitching eyes enchant the women who have looked down at her and they shower her with heaps of rags and tattered clothing. In an instant she has melted away, vanished. You don't know: has she flown off or has the earth swallowed her up?

And here is a blind vendor of mixed condiments, who will not sell to you unless you first greet him, when he will recite to you the legal formula for buying and selling.

The day draws to a close and the vendor of pickles takes his leave with his barrels, and the feet of the man with the foot-lathe leave their daily work and their tools to take their owner off home. The tram remains a rapacious beast, claiming its daily toll. The evening draws on, freshened by a diffident breeze. Soft laughter mingles with the harsh guffaws of men high on hashish. If you turn off the square into the entrance to Marasina Street you will hear the uproar of drunks in the Anastasi Bar, which the locals have nicknamed the "Have a Good Time" Bar. A drunk emerges from it, raging and staggering and accosting the passersby:

"Show me the toughest guy around here."

"Get lost, you so-and-so."

"Let him be, poor wretch."

"May God forgive him."

The sorrowful, tired specters of the square are now stirred by some sort of delight and merriment. There is no care in the world, and the future is in the hands of God. Faces come close together in affection and the person in pain forgets to complain, and a man will spend the last of his money on a narghile or a game of cards. Let come what may! The sounds of the clashing of the scales of a balance grow less, the hand-carts disappear, the candles are being put out inside the baskets. It is now that Ismail's walk around the square comes to an end. He is familiar with every corner, every inch, every stone. No vendor's call is new to him, nor the place from which it comes. The crowds enfold him and he is like a drop of rain that is swallowed up by the ocean. So used to the ever-recurring, ever-similar images, they find not the least response within him; he is neither curious nor bored, knowing neither contentment nor anger. He is not sufficiently detached for his eye to take them in. Who will say to him that all these sounds he hears and of which he is unaware, all these forms his eye alights on and which he does not see, that all these have an extraordinary power to creep into the heart, to penetrate stealthily, to establish themselves in it and to settle down in its very depths so that one day they will become his very substance? As for now, his glance picks out no particular aspect of life—all it has to do is to look.

As adolescence approached, he felt his body beginning to flare up, as though under some compulsion. He felt himself a prey torn between forces that were pulling him in opposite directions. He would flee from people and would go almost mad in his loneliness. He began to feel a strange delight in squeezing his way between the women who repaired to the mosque, in particular on special visiting days. In such a crowd the meaning of clothes for him was that they were partitions between naked bodies; these bodies he would sense from someone slightly brushing against him or from glancing contact. In the midst of these bodies he would have the pleasurable feeling of bathing in a flowing stream, unconcerned about the cleanness of the water: the smell of sweat and of scent did not put him off—rather he nosed them out like a dog. Visiting days were not without a few prostitutes, for Sidi al-Itris was ordered not to turn anyone away from the courtyard—people who came to light a candle at the shrine, or to fulfil their vows, hoping that God might grant them repentance and erase from their foreheads the destiny imprinted there. Though he had seen them before, he had not been aware of them; now, however, he followed them, his gaze fixed lingeringly on them. He paid particular attention to a girl with a dark complexion, curly hair, and fine lips who used to come on every visiting day. Her name was Naima and she differed from her companions in her silence and her slender build. All of them walked in an abandoned, loosely indifferent manner, whereas she made her way as though bent on some purpose, in possession of her being and her soul. Her arms were held straight against her sides, the inside of the elbow facing forward. If you looked carefully you would find nothing of the prostitute about her apart from two arms that had been broken by her fall, whereas the others appeared to have the idea that flexing of the arm was the secret of licentiousness.

Ismail smiled when he saw Sheikh Dardiri, the attendant of the shrine, amid the women, like a cock among hens. He knew them one by one and inquired about those who were absent. He would take a candle from this one and make way for another one to proceed to the donations box. His good will would change all of a sudden and he would scold them and push them outside. Men and women would also come to him asking for a little of the oil from the lamp of Umm Hashim to treat their eyes or the eyes of those dear to them. The holy oil would cure those whose perception shone brightly with faith, for there was no restoration of sight without such inner perception. And it was no fault of the oil if someone was not cured; rather it was because Umm Hashim had not as yet extended her grace to him. Perhaps it was because of the sins he had committed, or because he had not yet been cleansed of filth and impurity, so he should bear himself in patience and wait, while continuing to pay regular visits to the shrine, for if patience is the basis of the struggle in this world, it was also the sole means of attaining the Hereafter.

This oil provided Sheikh Dardiri with an ample source of revenue. Even so, he bore no signs of well-being: his filthy gallabiya was ever the same, his dingy turban likewise. What did he do with his money? Did he store it away under some flagstone? His colleagues accused him of burning it all up in smoking hashish, citing as proof of this his perpetual cough and his propensity for joking and making puns. The fact of the matter was that he was a much-married man, hardly a year going by without him becoming betrothed to some new virgin.

Ismail came to know him through his frequent visits to the

shrine, and would pay him a visit most nights after the evening prayers to enjoy his conversation. The man took a liking to the young lad, and showed him particular affection, and it was this affection that prompted him one night to reveal to Ismail a secret he had divulged to no one else:

"You know, Ismail Effendi, that on the Night of the Presence, our Master Hussein comes, together with the Imam Shafi'i and the Imam al-Layth, and they surround the Lady Fatima al-Nabawiya, the Lady Aisha, and the Lady Sakina with a troop of cavalry. Above them are green banners, and the scent of musk and roses is diffused from the sleeves of their garments. They take their places to the right and left of each Lady and hold court in order to look into injustices against the people. If they so wished they could remove all wrongs, but the time for this has not yet come, for there is no one oppressed who is not also an oppressor. How, then, can a person be requited? On that night, this small lamp that you see above the shrine, with hardly any light issuing from it, will give forth a light that shines with blinding brilliance. At such times I cannot bear to bring my eyes up to it. On that night its oil has the secret power of healing, and so I give it only to those forlorn creatures whom I know deserve it."

Ismail was absentmindedly thinking of the dark girl who used to purse her lips. He came to himself to find Sheikh Dardiri pointing at the lamp, drowsy like the tranquil eyes that have seen, have comprehended, and have come to rest. It casts its dim light over the shrine like the radiance of a mother's comely face as she gives nourishment from her breast to her babe so that it may find sleep in her embrace— the flickerings of the wick like her heartbeats of tenderness, or like the stations of her whispered glorification that float above the shrine, just as its guardian reverently keeps his distance. As for the chain, it is sheer illusion and pretence. Every light denotes a clash between a cowering darkness and a propulsive luminosity—all except for this lamp, which glows without struggle! There is no east here, no west, no day and no night, no yesterday and no tomorrow.

A shudder went through Ismail, without him knowing what it was that had touched his heart.

His puberty coincided with the year of the baccalaureate. Ismail came out of the examination with a heart agitated and brimful of doubts. When the results were announced, he found that, while he had passed, he had come low down in the lists.

His own hope and his whole family's wish had been that he would enter the Faculty of Medicine, but now its doors were closed to him. The new year approached, and he came to no decision. He had no choice but to enter the Teacher Training College or to study for the baccalaureat again and waste a year of his life. Both alternatives were equally distasteful to him. Sheikh Ragab was no less upset and anxious than his son. Some of his acquaintances expected that he would consider his son's education so far sufficient and find him some post with his matriculation, if not to help him but at least to lighten his burden. If only they had known how determined Sheikh Ragab was to push his son into the front ranks! He sought here and there for some sort of solution to the problem. I don't know who it was who said to him, "Why not send your son to Europe?"

Sheikh Ragab spent the night tossing and turning in his bed. He knew that this plan would cost him a large month-

ly sum, quite apart from the initial expenses of travel and of
clothes to protect Ismail against the cold of the north. Also,
could he bear to part from his son? Would his mother agree
or would her tender love for him stand in the way of Ismail's
future? Was he able to afford to pay such a sum regularly
every month? Were he to do so, the family would be left to
live on a mere pittance. And for how long? For six or seven
years—and time could be cruel and turn against him. He
heard both the call to evening prayers and the call to dawn
prayers; only then did he drift into a brief sleep, during
which he heard a gentle voice call out to him: "Put your
trust in God."

He awoke with his mind made up. The mother, realizing
that separation was inevitable, consented silently, though
she never ceased her weeping. Where to? Foreign parts! The
phrase, with a magical ring about it, crept its way, like a
cryptic spirit, into the house where the reciting of the
Qur'an never stopped and where the canonical law of Islam
represented the whole of truth and knowledge. This spirit
had taken up residence in a small corner of the house, had
covered its head and stretched out its body and had tri-
umphantly fallen into a gratified slumber. Foreign parts! The
father would pronounce the phrase as though it were some
form of charity from an infidel that he had no choice but to
accept. As for the mother, from this time on she was over-
taken by the terrors of the sea and a cold shivering. She
imagined 'foreign parts' as being at the end of a tall stairway
that ended at a land covered in snow and inhabited by peo-
ples who possessed the wiles and tricks of the djinn. As for
Fatima al-Nabawiya, her heart was in a flutter, for she had
heard that the women of Europe went about half naked and
that they were all highly skilled in the ways of enticement

and seduction. If Ismail were to travel there, you wouldn't know in what state he would return, if at all.

The father collected together all the money he could, and the mother sold her jewelry. And so the tickets were bought, as well as the thick clothes that would protect him against the cold of Europe.

With the approach of the date of departure, the time for saying goodbye arrived. The family collected, silent and sad, with trembling hearts and tearful eyes.

"My advice to you," the father addressed his son, "is that you live in foreign parts as you live here and that you are scrupulous about your religion and its duties. If you once become negligent about them you don't know where that will lead you. We want you, my son, to return to us a success, so that you may show us in a favorable light in front of people. I am a man who is on the threshold of old age and I have placed all our hopes in you. Beware of the women of Europe, that they don't lead you astray, for they are not for you and you are not for them."

The father was silent for a while, then continued. "You should know that your mother and I have agreed that Fatima al-Nabawiya should wait for you, for you are the person most worthy of her and she of you. She is your cousin and has no one but you. If you like, we shall read the Fatiha together today, so that blessings and good fortune may accompany you on your journey."

Ismail could only agree. He put his hand in that of his father and read the opening chapter of the Qur'an with him, while between them a mother wept and a young girl was at a loss to know whether to be joyful or sad.

Ismail had known that this reading of the Qur'an would one day come about, but he had not expected it to occur that very night. He had been brought up with Fatima al-Nabawiya as though they were brother and sister; seldom had he glanced at her in the way he had at the dark-skinned girl.

It was in a distraught state that he recited the Fatiha in order to please his father. His heart was saying to him, "Keep to your moral pledge." And he would answer it, "Why? Why?" Such matters were a mystery to him, for he was still pure and chaste, still had not known a woman. Yet he would be lying—and Ismail was no liar—were he to deny that he hungered after his dark-skinned girl, for women in general, and especially for the women of Europe!

Ismail went to say goodbye to some of his friends, then ended up in the square as sunset approached. His ears caught what they could of the vendors' cries with which he was familiar. It appeared to him that there was something unusual in the movement of people, as if they were quicker in their gait. Why was it that they weren't paying attention to anything? Was not life, then, but a race? How he wished that one of those who was charging ahead would stop and exchange some words with him. But no one paid him any heed. In the square people moved about like ants in lines that ran parallel and crossed in every direction.

His feet led him to the shrine, which he found unusually quiet. Sheikh Dardiri was standing with bowed head, as though exhausted or overcome by awesome fear. Ismail walked round the shrine until he came to the wall separating the place for the women from the men. He noticed a figure standing behind him: it was his dark-skinned girl, who was resting her forehead against the railing. Ismail, rooted to the spot, heard her say in a whisper, "O Umm Hashim, O you who shield women, deflect not your gaze, turn not your face away. The hand of one who seeks mercy is stretched toward you, so take hold of it. God has purified you, has sustained you and has put you down in His garden, and your heart is compassionate. If the sick, the defeated, and the broken have not sought you, then who else should they seek? If we have been forgotten, let you at least remember! When will that which has been destined for me be wiped out? Here is my soul at your threshold, felled to the ground, twisting and writhing and wanting to recover. Since God's grace has left me, I have been like someone asleep and pursued by nightmares, clutching at life and death with a single hand! I consented to His judgment and handed myself over, and I shall not be lost so long as you are here with us. Will it be long, or is God's mercy close at hand? I have made a solemn vow to you that the day when the Lord shall make me turn from sin I shall decorate your holy shrine with candles, with fifty candles, O Umm Hashim, O sister of al-Husayn."

The girl placed her lips against the railing of the shrine. This kiss was not part of her trade, it came from the heart. Who is there who would assert for certain that Umm Hashim had not herself come to the railing, her lips ready to exchange kiss for kiss?

Ismail decided to leave the mosque to catch her up and speak to her, yet his feet did not move. He wanted to unburden himself to her of everything inside himself. The moment of knowing that he would be torn from his family and his country to face loneliness and the unknown living in a strange land had frayed his nerves and broken his heart. Why was he so agitated when he saw her rather than other

women? Was he fantasizing? No. There was a hidden voice
inside his heart that wanted to make itself heard, to speak
and guide him to the secret, yet a thousand and one cover-
ings hid this voice and rendered it inaudible. Perhaps the
girl had not seen him, was not aware of his presence. Ismail
fled from his bewilderment to Sheikh Dardiri, whose loqua-
ciousness rained down on his heart like a balm. Standing
there in the silence of the shrine and under the light of the
lamp, his hand occasionally grasping hold of the railing, at
other times passing across his face—these were the last
things he remembered about his departure from Cairo.

All that happened to him after leaving the shrine
enveloped him from tip to toe, like a fierce precipitous current. Time lost its routine, visible things their normality,
and sounds their veracity and diversity. How bitter were his
farewells with his family! First of all in the house amid wail-
ing and sobbing, then at the station and on the train, then
at the port with its bustle, with the unknown ship and its
hooting. I can imagine him going up the gangway as a
young man but with the gravity of a sheikh, slow-moving,
staid, a little naive, everything about him giving the impression of a lonesome villager in the city. My uncle Ismail later
swore to me that he carried a pair of wooden slippers in his
luggage, for Sheikh Ragab had heard that making one's ablu-
tions before prayers in Europe was rendered difficult by the
fact that people had the habit of wearing their shoes indoors.
He also described to me, smilingly, the length and breadth
of the baggy Mahallawi underpants with the waistband he
was wearing. He even took with him a basketful of peasant
cakes and pastries that had been baked for him by his mother and Fatima al-Nabawiya.

And so the ship sailed away.

Seven years passed before the boat returned.

Who was that smart, tall, upstanding young man with radiant face and head held high who came down the gangway in leaps and bounds? By God, it was none other than Ismail, or rather—begging his pardon—Dr. Ismail, the eye specialist to whose singular distinction and rare brilliance the universities of England had testified. His professor used to joke with him and say, "I bet the spirit of some pharaonic doctor priest has materialized in you, Mr. Ismail. Your country is in need of you, for it is the land of the blind."

He had seen knowledge in him that was as though instinctual, and a clarity of vision that was descended from the maturity of long generations, and a nimbleness in his fingers that had been inherited from the same hands that had carved from solid stone effigies that were almost alive.

Come along, Ismail, for we are looking forward to having you back. For seven years that have passed like centuries we have not seen you.

Your regular letters, which became less frequent, were not sufficient to quench our burning longing for you. Come to us, as welcome as good health and rain, and take your place in the family, for you will find that it has become like a machine that has rusted up and come to a stop because its engine has been wrenched from it. What sacrifices this family has made for you! Do you realize?

The night before his arrival, Ismail slept spasmodically. At dawn he hurried up on deck, not wanting to miss the first glimpse of the coast of Alexandria. Though he could see nothing on the horizon, his nostrils breathed in from the breeze an unfamiliar smell. The first thing he met from his homeland was a creature whose homeland was the whole universe: a white bird, which alone hovered around the ship, free, lonely, immaculate, sovereign. Why do ships deliberately dawdle on arriving? And yet how speedy is their departure! She was now taking her time, caring not at all for the feelings of her passengers. Ismail had kept the date of arrival from his family so as to spare his elderly father the trouble of making the journey to Alexandria. He intended to send them a telegram about the arrival of his train in Cairo.

Over there he could see the sea-girt lighthouse, and there the yellow shoreline that was almost on a level with the water. Egypt, you are like the palm of a hand stretched out into the sea, taking pride in nothing but its expansiveness. In front of you are no barriers of treacherous reefs, no impeding mountains on your shore. You are a home in which everything inspires one with a sense of security.

Here there appears the first small boat. In it, an old, white-bearded man squats like a monkey with bent back in the prow as he fishes. His gallabiya is blue—or was—and it is ragged and patched. Ismail's gaze falls on an Egyptian woman standing beside him; he sees her looking down at the fisherman, her eyes welling with tears. He hears her mutter, "Egypt! Egypt!"

How could the fisherman pay her attention when he was not even aware of the whole ship, of whose like there were many, coming in and going out and almost colliding with his small boat? His closed world was proof against the ship, his world that followed the same pattern day after day. Ismail thought to call out to this old man, to greet him or to wave to him with his handkerchief. How standards are allowed to fall away, logic to be defeated at such moments when emotions are ablaze and hearts unpolluted!

A bell rang, announcing the death of the ship; its corpse

became prey to an attack by an army of human ants: soldiers and officers, and our brethren the occupiers (even though mixed up among the others and tarbushed like them), as well as porters, money-changers, and visitors. Then the crowd and the jostling spilt forth, cries rang out, and there was much kissing and hugging, with Ismail in the midst of the current, unsubmerged by it, greedily gathering to himself all the impressions he could, on his lips a sweet smile of contentment, his ear was sharp and discerning, and with a lively, watchful gaze that wanted to see everything and to understand everything.

If you looked carefully at him you would find that the chubbiness of his face had disappeared and that his cheeks were tautened into two ridges. His lips, which used to be flabby and were seldom closed tight, were now set in an expression of confident determination. He passed through the customs, and in the carriage he listened to the rhythm of the wheels, sometimes on asphalt and sometimes on paving stones, and the shifting discord reminded him of the day he set out on his journey. How distantly set in a deep abyss of the past did it appear to him today, as distant as a dream . . . . How does a day's memory have the strength to survive after seven years spent in England, seven years that had turned his life upside down? He had been chaste and had been led astray, had been sober and had got drunk, had danced with young girls and had misbehaved. This degeneration was equaled by an improvement that was no less serious and curious: he had learned how to appreciate nature's beauty, to enjoy sunsets—as though there were not in his own country sunsets that were no less beautiful—and how to find pleasure in the sting of the cold of the north.

If during this period he had had nothing but Mary, his fellow student, it would have sufficed to make him forget his past. This dark eastern youth had captivated her heart and she had fallen for him and had embraced him to her. When she had given herself to him, it was she who had deprived him of his virginal innocence. She had removed him from a state of unhealthy lethargy to one of confident energy, and she had opened up to him new horizons of beauty of which he had been ignorant: in art, in music, and in nature, even in the human soul.

One day he said to her, "I shall rest only when I have laid down a program for my life along which I can proceed."

She had laughed and replied, "My dear Ismail, life is no fixed program, but an ever renewed debate."

He would say to her, "Let's sit down," and she would say to him, "Come on, let's walk."

He would talk to her of marriage, and she would talk to him of love. He would talk to her of the future, she to him of the present moment. Previously he had been looking outside himself for something to cling to, to lean on: his religion and his faith, his upbringing and his roots, which for him were like a hook on which to hang his expensive overcoat. But she would say to him, "He who resorts to a hook will remain his whole life a prisoner alongside it, guarding his overcoat. Your hook must be inside yourself." The thing she most feared were fetters, while the thing he most feared was freedom. The fact that she gave herself to him was, at the start, a source of bewilderment to him, and his bewilderment became a butt for her sarcasm. He used to shun people and would calculate the possibilities of their liking him and would be concerned about their judgment of him. If he found someone happy being amiable toward him, he found no harm in being civil to them, but his heart would not become engaged. Getting to know people was for him a clash between personalities from which one emerged either victorious or the loser. She, on the other hand, would be in raptures about everyone, but paid no heed to any of them. Getting to know people for her was meeting them, while affection was left to the future. While having equal affection for everyone, she was ruthless in distancing the weak, the stupid, the pretentious, the despicable, the mournful, and the hypocritical. Freeing herself from such worthless persons, she gravitated only to those in whose company she felt at ease.

She saw that he spent a lot of time with the weak among his patients, giving his special attention to those whose nerves and minds had been affected by the destructive effects of time—and how many such people there are in Europe! In silence he would sit and listen to their complaints. The greatest expression of generosity he showed was to align his own reasoning to their sick way of thinking. Mary saw the circle of the sick and the defeated closing in on him and clinging to him, each demanding him for himself, and she proceeded to awaken him forcibly.

"You are not the Messiah, the son of Mary. He who seeks the disposition of angels is overwhelmed by the disposition of beasts. Charity is to begin with yourself. These people are drowning and are searching for a hand to be held out to them. But if they find it, they let it drown with them. These oriental sentiments of yours are despicable and disgusting, because they are not practical or productive. If divested of usefulness, they can be labeled only as weak and contemptible. Strength with such emotions lies in concealing them, not in disclosing them."

His soul would moan and cringe under the blows of her axe. He would feel her words cutting into the living ligaments from which he fed when in contact with those around him. One day he woke up to find that his spirit was in ruins, not a single stone resting on another. Religion became for him a fable that had been invented in order to keep the masses in control, while the human spirit could find no strength, and thus no happiness, unless it detached itself from crowds and from confronting them; to immerse oneself in them was a weakness spelling disaster.

His nerves were unable to cope with this morass in which he found himself drowned and alone. He fell ill and broke off his studies. He was ravaged by a sort of anxiety and disquiet; in fact, flashes of fear and panic were sometimes to be seen in his eyes.

It was Mary who came to his rescue. She took him on a trip to the Scottish countryside. During the day they wandered around on foot or by bicycle; or they would go fishing; at night she would let him taste the pleasures of love in all its forms. He was fortunate to be able to pass through that crisis which afflicts many of his young compatriots when they are in Europe. He came through it with a new self, one that was stable and confident; if this new self had cast aside religious belief, it had substituted for it a stronger faith in science. He no longer thought of the blissful beauty of paradise but of the splendor of nature and its mysteries. Perhaps the best evidence of his cure was that he had begun to free himself from the hold Mary had over him. No longer did he sit before her like a disciple before his master, but as a colleague. He was not astonished, nor greatly hurt, when he saw her moving away from him and taking up with a fellow student of her own race and color—as with every artist she was growing bored with her work of art once it had been completed. Once cured, Ismail for her lost all his magic,

becoming just like the other people she knew. Let her then
try out her new friend. Ismail, however, did not have the
heart to leave England without attempting a final meeting
with her. He invited her, and she did not turn him down.
When she came, he did not ask himself whether it was with
the knowledge of her new friend or behind his back. And
once again she gave herself to him, for this joining was not
one of great moment for her: her embrace was a sort of
handshake, a way of saying goodbye.

As she went off on her bicycle she called out to him, "I
hope to see you in Egypt one of these days. Who knows?
Until we meet, then—I won't say goodbye."

Modern women! How they face up to possibilities with a
staunch heart! The path of life is before them, heavy with a
variety of fruit. They have a keen appetite, so why shed tears
of regret over a single fruit when the tree is overflowing?

The extraordinary thing I could not explain was that Ismail
recovered from his love for Mary to find himself a prey to a
new love. Is it that the heart cannot live untenanted? Or was
it that Mary had inadvertently caused his heart to wake up
and come to new life?

Ismail used to have only the vaguest of feelings for Egypt.
He was like a grain of sand that has been merged into other
sands and has become so assimilated among them that he
could not be distinguished from them even when separated
from all the other grains. Now, however, he felt himself to
be a ring in a long chain that tightly bound him to his
mother country. In his mind Egypt was like the forest bride
touched by the wand of a wicked witch that had sent her to
sleep. She was dressed in all her jewelry and finery for the

night of consummation. Cursed by God is the eye that cannot see her beauty and the nostril that cannot smell her perfume. When will she wake up? When? The stronger his love for Egypt grew, the greater his irritation with Egyptians. None the less they were his flesh and blood, and the fault was not theirs. They were the victims of ignorance, poverty, disease, and chronically long oppression. Many a time he had stared into the eyes of death, had handled leprosy, had put his mouth close to the mouth of someone in fever. Could it be that he would now flinch from touching this human mass when his flesh was part of theirs, his blood from theirs? He had pledged to himself, in his love for Egypt, that whatever objectionable thing he set his eyes on he would remove it. Mary had taught him to be self-dependent, and woe after that to whoever sought to feed him with their superstitions, fantasies, and customs. Not in vain had he lived in Europe and taken part in its prayers to science and logic. He knew that between him and those with whom he would come into contact there would be a long struggle, though his youth made him underrate the fight and its difficulties. In fact, he was already ardently yearning for the first battle. He let his mind wander and saw himself as a journalist writing in the newspapers or as an orator at a meeting expounding his views and beliefs to the masses.

The train moved off and he had not sent his telegram. He did not know why he shrank from meeting them at the station amid the clamor and bustle, the confusion of luggage, and under the gaze of other people. He wanted to meet his dear ones in their own home, far out of the sight of strangers. He did, however, appreciate the shock this would have on his father and his aged mother. When he thought of them his heart trembled: was he able to pay back some part of the debt he owed them? He was returning home equipped with the very weapon his father had wanted for him, and he was determined that with this weapon he would carve for himself a path to the front ranks. He would stay away from government service and would open his own clinic in the best district of Cairo. First of all, he would astonish the Cairenes, then the Egyptians in their entirety, with his skill and the breadth of his experience. When the money came pouring in, he would see to it that his old father would no longer have to work and he would buy him some land in their village so that he would be able to live in comfort. Ismail then brought himself up with a start as he remembered that he had brought no gifts with him from Europe for the family.

He consoled himself with the thought: "What is there in the whole of Europe that is good enough for my father and mother?"

And Fatima al-Nabawiya? The memory of her brought a certain feeling of discomfort. He was still bound by his promise: having returned a free man, he had no excuse to call it off. But this was a complex matter and was best left to the future.

He looked out of the window and saw a moving landscape that appeared to have been coated by a sand storm, a landscape dilapidated, begrimed, and devastated. The vendors at the stations were in tattered clothes, pouring with sweat and panting like hunted animals.

When the horse-carriage he took from the station entered narrow Khalig Street, which was not wide enough for the tram to pass through, the sight that met his eyes was uglier than anything he had imagined: dirt and flies, poverty, and buildings in a state of ruin. He was overcome by depression, struck dumb by what he saw. The flame of revolt grew stronger within him, and he became more determined than ever to gird himself for action.

Standing before the house, he took hold of the knocker and let it fall back. Its knock mingled with the beatings of his heart. He heard a gentle voice calling in the tone used by the women of Cairo: "Who?"

"It's me—Ismail! Open the door, Fatima!"

O Ismail, how cruel you are! How callous is youth!

His mother almost fainted as, tongue-tied, she embraced him and kissed his face and hands, sobbing and weeping. Good God! How old she had become, how wasted, how weak her voice and eyesight! The absent man lives under an illusion, expecting that he will return to his dear ones and find them as he left them many years before. A voice whispered in his heart, "She has been stripped of all personality! She is nothing but a mass of passive goodness."

His father came to him, a quiet smile playing on his face. Though his head had turned grey, he was as upright as ever. In his eyes was a look that was a mix of composed exhaustion, ease of conscience, and the sensation of bearing a heavy burden. Ismail would later learn that he had fallen on bad times. Even so, he had not once been late in depositing the money for his son in the bank. He had not mentioned to Ismail what he was going through, nor had he asked him to be economical or to hurry back home. Ismail was having a good time in Scotland and eating steak, while his father was confined to the house and making his supper off radishes or taamiya.

Ismail cast a glance from the corner of his eye at the house and found that it was even more cramped and dingy than he remembered. Were they still getting their light from paraffin lamps? The dilapidated pieces of furniture that were scattered about—despite the passage of the years and the length of their association with the house—looked as though they had been dumped in some land of exile. Why were they standing on the stone floor? Where were the carpets?

There was Umm Mohamed dithering about as usual among the pots and pans as she let out trilling cries of joy at his return. He scolded her. "Don't make such a noise, woman. Be sensible."

But where was Fatima al-Nabawiya? When she came, he saw a young woman in the prime of youth; her two plaits of hair, her cheap glass bracelets, her movements, and everything about her proclaimed that she was a peasant girl from the depths of the countryside. Was this the girl he was going to marry? From that instant he knew that he would betray his promise and break his vow. And why were her eyes bandaged? In order to be able to see his face, she raised her chin. Since he had left she had continued to suffer from trachoma, her condition worsening day after day.

Supper was prepared and they sat down to it. Perhaps it was for his sake that they sat round a table made of white wood. No one ate: they did not eat because they were overjoyed, while he did not eat because of the shock of coming to his senses. Ismail was later to confess to me that even at the moment when the happiness of being back with his parents should have driven out thoughts of comparison and disparagement, he could not help asking himself how he would be able to live among them and be comfortable in this house.

His bed was made ready and Sheikh Ragab insisted on

retiring to his room so that his son might be left to rest from the fatigue of traveling. His mother, dragging herself away, was about to leave him when she pointed to Fatima and said, "Come here, Fatima, let me put some drops in your eyes before you go to sleep."

Ismail saw his mother with a small bottle in her hands, while Fatima sat on the floor and put her head on his mother's knee. When she poured some drops from the bottle into the girl's eyes, Fatima groaned with pain.

"What's that, mother?' asked Ismail.

"It's oil from the lamp of Umm Hashim. Every evening I pour some of it into her eyes. Your friend Sheikh Dardiri brought it to us. He remembers you and longs to see you again. Do you remember him, or have you forgotten him?"

As if bitten by a snake, Ismail jumped to his feet. Was it not extraordinary that on the very first night of his return he should be witnessing—he an eye doctor—the way diseases of the eye were treated in his home country?

Ismail went to Fatima and made her stand up. Removing the bandage, he examined her eyes. He found that the disease had destroyed the eyelids and had harmed the eye itself. If the right soothing treatment were applied, her eyes would regain their health, but they were only made worse by the hot, stinging oil.

"You should be ashamed of yourself at the harm you're doing," he shouted at his mother at the top of his voice. "Shame on you! And you a believer who says her prayers, how can you accept such superstitions and humbug?"

His mother was tongue-tied and kept silent. Though she tried to mutter something not a word came out.

Ismail saw his father's form at the door: he was in a short gallabiya, his face ashen under the skull-cap that covered his head. Did his gentle heart expect that something unpleasant was about to happen? But what? Perhaps there was something about Ismail's behavior, his movements and expression, that awakened certain apprehensions in him from the very first moment. What was this shouting? What had happened?

At last his mother pronounced the words, "I take my refuge in God," and then said to him, "God protect you, my son Ismail. May the Lord keep you in your right mind. This is nothing to do with medicine, though. This is just the blessing of Umm Hashim."

Ismail was like an enraged bull at whom a red rag is being waved.

"So this is your Umm Hashim, the one that will make the girl blind! You'll see how I'll treat her and how I'll cure her when Umm Hashim failed."

"My son, many people seek blessings through the oil of Umm Hashim, the Mother of the Destitute. They tried it, and the Lord cured them through it. All our life, it is God and Umm Hashim that we put our trust in. Her secret powers are invincible."

"I know neither Umm Hashim nor Umm of the Fairies!"

A grave-like silence of despondency descended on the house inhabited by readings from the Qur'an and the echo of calls to prayer. It was as though all these had woken up, sprung into life, and then been extinguished, only to be replaced by a gloomy darkness. There was no life for this house now that this strange spirit had come to it from across the seas.

He heard his father's voice as though it came to him from some faraway place. "What are you saying? Is this what you learned abroad? Is all we have gained to have you return to us an infidel?"

Everything Ismail did after this showed that his old psy-

chological malaise had suddenly come back to him. Once
again, he exploded violently. Losing control of himself, he
felt the dryness in his throat, the burning in his chest, and a
head that was swimming in some world other than this one.
He jumped to his feet. No doubt there was something
frightening about his expression, for his mother cringed
away from him and his father drew to one side. Throwing
himself at his mother, he tried to wrench the bottle from
her. For a moment she clung to it, then she let it go. He
snatched it from her roughly and with a quick movement
flung it from the window.

The sound of it smashing in the street was the blast of the
first bomb in a battle.

For a moment Ismail stood in a daze. He glanced at his
family around him, his gaze traveling from the faces of his
mother and Fatima to that of his father. Though he found
pity and sympathy, he did not find compliance and understanding. Perhaps, too, he detected in their eyes a certain
flicker of terror. His agitation increasing, he rushed to the
door. On the way out he found his father's walking stick.
Taking it up, he ran out of the house. He would not flinch
from delivering a *coup de grâce* to the very heart of ignorance
and superstition, be it the last thing he did.

He drew near the square and found it as usual surging with
myriad creatures. All bore traces of misery, their feet as
though shackled with servility and oppression. These were
not living creatures existing in an age when even inanimate
objects moved; these multitudes of people were broken,
empty relics like the stumps of pedestals of ruined columns,
with no purpose in life except to be objects against which

the feet of passersby would stumble. What was this animal clamor? What was this lowly food which so many mouths were gobbling down? He looked at the faces and saw nothing but traces of a deep foundering in sleep, as though they were all under the thrall of opium. Not a single face gave expression to a human concept. These are the Egyptians: an uncouth, garrulous race, scurfy and sore-eyed, naked and barefoot, with blood in its urine and worms in its excrement; it accepts the slap on the back of its long neck with a fawning smile that breaks across the whole face. And Egypt? Nothing but a sprawling piece of mud that had dozed off in the middle of a desert. Above it were clouds of flies and mosquitoes, with a herd of emaciated water buffaloes submerged up to their flanks in mud.

The square thronged with people selling salted sunflower seeds and broad beans, earth almonds and the pastries known as the umda's cudgel, hareesa, baseesa, and sanbuska, all sold for paltry sums. Along its sides were numerous cafés spreading onto the sidewalks and against the walls, their mainstay a brazier, a water jug, and the narghile, and bodies that have not known water for years, and for which soap and the phoenix are equally mysterious.

A girl passed before him, with penciled eyebrows and with kohl around her eyes, her milaya tightly wound about her to accentuate her buttocks and show off the edge of her dress, her veil revealing her face. And what was the purpose of this brass tube she wore on her nose? How disgusting! How ugly and repugnant was the sheer hypocrisy of the sight of her! Soon men began rubbing themselves against her, like dogs that had never seen a bitch. Here was the inertia that would kill all progress, a nothingness where time had no meaning, the fantasies of the drugged, the dreams of the sleeper when the sun has risen. Had he been able to, Ismail would have seized the arm of every one of them and given it a good shake.

"Wake up!" he would have said. "Wake up from your slumber, come to, and open your eyes. What is this useless dispute? This prattling and altercation about trifling matters? You live in a world of fables and you believe in idols, you make pilgrimages to graves and you seek refuge with the dead."

His foot stumbled against a child lying on the sidewalk, while around him were crowds of beggars, exposing to his gaze their deformities from which they derived an honest living; it was as though these deformities were blessings bestowed upon them by God, or as if they constituted normal trades and skills.

Ismail felt that these hordes of people were dead limbs weighing down on his chest, stifling him, tearing at his nerves. Some passersby collided with him like blind people groping about in their darkness. This acceptance was mere incompetence, this goodness stupidity, this patience cowardice, this gaiety degeneracy.

Ismail slipped away from the crowd and ran to the mosque. He went through the courtyard to the shrine. The tomb breathed in—in place of air—the heavy fumes of barbaric perfumes. Over there hung the lamp, dust clinging to its glass, its chain blackened with soot. It gave off a choking stench of burning, for it emitted more smoke than light. Its thin ray of light was a standing advertisement to superstition and ignorance. In the roof a bat fluttered and he shuddered in disgust. Around the tomb stood people like wooden props, paralyzed, clinging to its railings. Among them was a man beseeching something of the lady who lay buried there, something that

Ismail did not understand, though he had the impression that he was inciting her against some enemy of his, asking her to bring ruin upon his house and render his children orphans.

Ismail turned to a corner of the shrine, where he found Sheikh Dardiri handing a small bottle to a man whose head was bandaged with a woman's kerchief; he did it surreptitiously, as though he were handling smuggled goods. Ismail could not control himself as he felt the clanging of a thousand bells in his head. With staring eyes, he raised his stick and brought it down on the lamp. As it was smashed and the pieces were scattered around, he screamed: "I . . . I . . . I . . . ."

He was unable to complete the sentence—and who knows what he was going to say? The crowds rushed at him and he fell to the ground in a faint. They hit him and trod him underfoot. The blood poured down his face from a wound in his head, and his clothes were torn to pieces.

We later learned that he would have died under their feet had it not been that Sheikh Dardiri recognized him and rescued him from the angry and violent mob.

"Leave him!" he said. "I know the man—it's Ismail, the son of Sheikh Ragab. He's one of us. Let him be. Don't you see he's possessed?"

They carried him home and put him to bed. The family gathered around him in a night of joy at his return as they wept for the loss of his reason.

God curse the day on which you voyaged away to Europe, Ismail! If only you had stayed among us and Europe had not corrupted you so that you lost your reason and insulted your people, your country, and your religion!

The mother slapped her face and the father groaned and curbed his pain and rage, while Fatima shed copious tears.

Many days passed and Ismail did not leave his bed. Driven by stubbornness, he turned his face to the wall, spoke to no one, and made no demands. When he had recovered slightly, he began to ask himself whether he should return to Europe, in order to live among people who understood what life was about. The university had offered him the post of assistant professor and he had stupidly refused the appointment, but perhaps they would accept him now if he were to ask. Why should he not marry over there and build himself a family under a new sky far away from this ill-fated land? Why had he left England, with its beautiful countryside, its pleasant evenings, and the terrible severity of its winter, to come to this land where people flee from a little drizzle as though threatened by some disastrous flood? Did they not know that in England people with solemn faces and impassive expressions walked calmly under rain, snow, and storms? What was the point of struggling in a country like Egypt and with a people like the Egyptians, who had lived under oppression for such long centuries that they had begun to savor it and even to find it sweet-tasting?

He was then overcome by sleep. He became confused, like a bird that has fallen into a trap. They had put him into a cage—was there some way out of it? He felt that his body was bound to this house he could not bear, to this square he loathed, and that however much he tried he would be unable to set himself free.

Ismail woke up one morning feeling imbued with extraordinary energy. In such circumstances a person leaps from one extreme to another, suddenly and without any apparent reason. He left the house early and came back carrying a bag full of bottles, bandages, and appliances for treating eyes. He began his treatment of Fatima as required by his medicine and its science. In Europe he had treated more than a hundred similar cases and not once had he failed. So why should he not succeed with Fatima too? The girl gave herself over to him calmly, concerned not so much with her disease as with being the object of his attention and kindness. His father and mother avoided him and no longer opposed him in anything, out of fear for his health.

In the morning and before going to bed, Fatima would place herself at his disposal. The days passed by, then a week and another week, with no change in Fatima's eyes, then suddenly they grew worse and became inflamed, and the white began to flow over into the black of the eye.

Ismail doubled his care and repeated the treatment with various kinds of medicine. He turned her eyelids up and applied drops and ointment, and he scraped and cleaned, but his treatment did no good. He saw that Fatima was on the way to becoming blind, and that his knowledge had been of no avail.

He took her to his colleagues at the Faculty of Medicine, where she was examined by the professors. They all agreed with his method of treatment and advised him to continue with it.

He persisted and persevered until finally Fatima woke up one morning to open her eyes and see nothing. Her last comforting glimmer of light had been extinguished.

Ismail fled from the house, unable to live in it with Fatima continually before him, her blindness a symbol of his own. The eyes of his father and mother were a reproach to him. What had happened? Why had he failed? He understood nothing. Where should he go? He had not yet started any work: he was neither capable of soliciting the government for an appointment in some faraway village, nor did he have any desire to do so. Selling his books and some of his instruments he had brought with him from Europe, he took a small room in the pension of Madame Eftalia, a portly Greek woman who, from the first moment he fell into her clutches, began to exploit him to such an extent that she almost charged him for her "Good morning," or for getting up to open the door to him. On one occasion she actually charged him for an extra lump of sugar he had taken with his breakfast. When she smiled he felt as though fingers were searching out his pockets. One day he made her a present of some pastries and cigarettes; she accepted them greedily and the very next morning asked him not to sit up so late in his room because of the electricity. There was no doubt in his mind that the Europeans to be found in Egypt were of a different mold from those he had known in Europe. He was accustomed to shut himself up in his room, but this behavior of hers drove him out into the streets, where he would wander about from morning until midnight. Every evening—he did not know how—he would find himself in the middle of the square, roaming around his own house, gazing in at the windows, hoping to see Fatima's face or hear her voice—Fatima who, having been his victim, had not rebelled against him, had not doubted, had not blamed him. She had given herself up to him of her own volition and he had repaid her by harming her. Yet she had never asked her butcher to bide his time.

And so he would remain standing for long hours in the square in a state of absentminded listlessness, with the old street cries filtering through to his ears; the very same, unchanged since his childhood. How was this? Perhaps because every father passed his trade on to his son, along with his voice and his place in the square. Poor wretches, he thought. Everyone who had ever done them a service had reminded them of it and had demanded quick repayment many times over. No one had served them out of charity, for the mere love of it, or for love of them. And yet they had run behind anyone they imagined to be sincere toward them and had clung to his coat tails. They had refused to recognize his weakness or treachery. This was a people who had grown old and reverted to childhood. Were they to find someone to lead them, they would spring back to a state of vigor once again at a single bound, for the road was familiar, and their ancient glories and old memories were intact.

Ismail asked himself: In the whole of Europe is there a square the like of Sayyida Zaynab? Europe had beautiful and magnificent buildings of high artistic standard, but it also had many people who were alone and lonely, fighting tooth and nail, stabbing each other in the back, and indulging in exploitation in its every form. The place for love and kind-liness was after work, at the end of the day. For them these emotions were forms of relaxation, like going to the theater and the cinema.

But no, he told himself, were he to surrender himself to such a way of thinking he would be refuting his mind and his knowledge. Who can deny Europe's civilization and progress, and the ignorance, disease, and poverty of the east? History had passed its verdict and there was no going back on that verdict, no way of denying that we are a tree that flourished and bore fruit for a time and then withered. It is quite unthinkable that life might invade it anew.

Ismail would flee from the square to his room and spend

the night thinking how he might escape back to Europe, but it would not be long before he returned to his accustomed place in the square the following night.

When the month of Ramadan came, it did not occur to him to fast. He began to stay longer in the square and to reflect on things: there was something new in the air, in the living beings and in the stones, something that was not there before. It was as though existence had cast off its old robe and garbed itself in a new one. The universe was overspread by an atmosphere of truce following a bitter battle.

Ismail questioned himself: Why had he failed? He had returned from Europe with a large quiver stuffed with knowledge, and yet when he examined it now he found it to be empty. It had no answer to his question. There it was in front of him, feeble and dumb; suddenly, despite its lightness, it had grown heavy in his hand.

He looked around him in the square, his gaze lingering on the masses. He found that he could tolerate them, and he began smiling at some of the jokes and laughter that reached his hearing, and these and the street calls took him back to the days of his childhood. He did not think there was a people like the Egyptians, with their ability to retain their distinctive character and temperament despite the vicissitudes of the times and the change of rulers. It all passed in front of the average Cairene like something out of the pages of al-Gabarti's chronicles. Ismail began to be at peace with himself and to feel that there was solid ground under his feet. There were no longer hordes of individuals in front of him but a whole people united together by a common bond, a sort of faith, the fruit of a close association with time and a long process of maturity. At this, the faces began to speak to him anew with meanings he had previously not noticed. Here was an arrival of tranquility and peace, and the sword was sheathed. In Europe, activity was undertaken in a state of anxiety and agitation, with the sword ever drawn. But why should one compare? The lover does not measure or compare: if comparison enters by the door, love takes flight out of the window.

Then came the Night of Power, that celebrated the night on which the Qur'an was revealed. Ismail was aware of it, and in his heart there was a strange longing for it. He had been brought up to venerate that night and to believe in its particular merits and its special standing among nights. He did not feel on any other night—not even those of the Feast—the same sensations of humility and piety toward God. In his mind it was a white blaze amid the blackness of nights. How many times on that night had he raised his glance to the sky and been entranced by its beauty, something of which he had not been aware for the remainder of the year.

For a while his thoughts strayed. Then his attention was drawn to the sound of a deep, moaning exhalation coursing through the square. It was doubtless Sidi al-Atris. He raised his gaze and saw the dome as though swinging in a deluge of light. Ismail was shaken from tip to toe. "O light, where have you been all this time? Welcome back! The veil that had descended over my heart and eyes has been raised. Now I understand what had been hidden from me. There is no knowledge without faith. She didn't believe in me; her whole faith was directed to your blessing, your loftiness, and your gracious favor, O Umm Hashim."

Ismail entered to the shrine with bowed head. He saw it dancing in the light of the fifty candles with which it had been decorated. Sheikh Dardiri was taking them one by one from a tall, dark-complexioned girl with curly hair. It was Nai'ma, the girl he had yearned for, years before. She no longer had pursed lips but a shining face, with teeth, when she smiled, that were as white as pearls; a mere look at her made one forget all the ugliness in the world.

She had lived in patience and faith and God had restored her to His grace. She had come to fulfill the vow she had made seven years ago. She had not despaired or rebelled or lost hope in God's generosity.

As for himself, the intelligent, educated, and cultured young man, he had grown proud and had rebelled, and his pride had taken a fall.

Ismail raised his gaze and saw the lamp in its place like a contented eye that viewed all, understood, and was at peace. It seemed to him that the lamp was signaling to him and smiling.

Sheikh Dardiri came to him to ask after his health and to hear his news.

"This is a blessed night, Sheikh Dardiri," Ismail said to him. "Give me some of the oil of the lamp."

"By God, you are in luck. Is it not the Night of Power, and the Night of the Presence as well?"

Ismail went out of the mosque carrying the bottle. Talking to himself, he spoke to the square and its people. "Come to me, all of you. Some of you have done me harm, and some of you have lied to me and cheated me, yet even so there is still a place in my heart for your filth, your ignorance, and your backwardness, for you are of me and I am of you. I am the son of this quarter, the son of this square. Time has been cruel to you, and the more cruel it is the stronger my affection is for you."

Entering the house, he called out to Fatima, "Come here, Fatima. Do not despair of being cured. I have brought you the blessings of Umm Hashim. She will drive away your illness and restore your sight as good as new."

He pulled at her plait of hair as he continued to speak. "And on top of that, I'll teach you how to eat and drink, how you should sit, and how you should dress—I'll make a lady of you."

He went back again to his medicine and science. But now he was given the support of faith. He did not despair when he found that the disease had taken a strong hold on her and none of his efforts seemed to have any effect. He persevered and went on treating her until there was a faint ray of hope, after which Fatima continued to improve daily, making up at the end of her treatment for the lack of any advance at the beginning. Finally, her progress went ahead in great leaps.

When, one day, he saw her standing in front of him in perfect health, he searched in vain in his mind and heart for the feeling of surprise that he feared would be there.

Ismail opened his own clinic in the district of al-Baghghala, close by the hills there, in a house quite unsuitable for receiving patients with eye complaints. His fee per visit never exceeded one piaster. Among his clients there were no well-dressed men and women, all were poor and barefooted. The strange thing was that his fame became established in the villages surrounding Cairo rather than in Cairo itself. His clinic was crammed with peasant men and women who would bring him gifts of eggs and honey, chickens and ducks.

He performed many a difficult operation using methods that would have left a European doctor aghast. He held closely to the spirit and basic principles of the science of medicine and abandoned all extremes of treatment and instruments. He relied first and foremost upon God, then on his knowledge and the skill of his hands—and God blessed his learning and his skill.

He had no wish to amass wealth, to put up blocks of flats, or to buy land. His sole aim was that his poor patients should find health at his hands.

Ismail married Fatima and she bore him five sons and six daughters.

Toward the end of his days he became extremely corpulent: he was a greedy eater and was full of laughter and joking. His clothes were shabby, with ash spread over his sleeves and trousers from the cigarettes that he chain-smoked. He became asthmatic, with a flushed face and a forehead that was damp with sweat, while his breathing became wheezy. Whoever looked at him was at a loss to know whether he was tired or relaxed. When his laughter was imprisoned in his throat it gathered in his eyes, for there are no eyes more expressive than the eyes of those who suffer from their chest: a merry devil seems to leap out of them at you, full of affection and understanding, of wicked playfulness and goodness, of tolerance and kindliness, as though, more than anything, it were saying to you, "There is more to existence than just you and me. There is beauty and secrets, enjoyment and magnificence. Happy the man who senses them. It is up to you to search them out . . . ."

Until now the people of the Sayyida district remember him with kindness and gratitude, then ask God to forgive him his sins. What sins? No one told me of any because of the deep affection they bore him. Nevertheless, I understood from significant looks and smiles that my uncle had had a love of women throughout his life. It was as if this love was an aspect of his dedicated love for humankind as a whole.

May God have mercy on him.